Cora

R. I. Poslgrove

Trigger Warnings!

Death

Abuse

Gore

VIolence

Murder

Religion/Religious Abuse

Illness

Thank you...

Matt, for being the best husband in the world!

Heidi, for being an incredible editor!

Jennifer Anne, for being so supportive!

Thank you to the wonderful people who let me use their pets as inspiration...

Chili and his parent, Dulce.

Edwin and Rosa Bud and their parent Beverly

Moe and his parents Ahlayna Davis and Nick McPherson

Elizabeth and her parent Bryanna

Rexi and Bear and their parent Kam

Princess Isabel and Admiral Sterling and their parent Anna McFencer

Astrix and his parent Elz Dobson

And thank you to Betty and her parent Bridget Richardson!

Dedicated to the Church

I have heard time and time again that there is no "one church." However, I have also heard the Nicene Creed spoken in churches of many different denominations. The last section of the prayer says:

*We believe in **one** holy Christian* (or catholic, meaning universal, not the Catholic denomination) *and apostolic **Church**.*
We acknowledge one baptism for the forgiveness of sins.
We look for the resurrection of the dead
and the life of the world to come. Amen.

So just assume I'm speaking to the universal church referenced in the prayer, *except* the Catholic church. I have some different things to say to the Catholic church, but I feel it was more suited for Quinn's backstory.

Be better.

Stop talking about how broken the church is and fix it.

I know "not all churches" are bad, but even the "good" ones don't hold the bad ones accountable for misrepresenting Christ.

The shame that is heaped on the heads of abuse victims is vile. Shunning people of the LGBTQ+ community is awful and cruel.

"But the church is a hospital for the broken!" Hospitals are where people go to be healed. They don't keep you sick. And being "sick" isn't an excuse for poor behavior.

4

"But we need to use tough love!" No, you don't. Bullying under the guise of tough love is abuse and coercion.

Of course, you are free to believe what you want. If you think someone is living in sin, fine. But that doesn't give you a pass to treat them like garbage. It doesn't make their life choices your business. And if you choose to lecture them on how much of a sinner they are, don't be surprised when it's not received well.

There are loads of people who have very justified hate of the church. If you don't like people calling the church out on its bullshit, stop hurting people.

Jesus says he loves everyone. Many Christians debate what that means, and it can get really complicated. I don't think Jesus was confused or being cryptic when he said to love others.

1 Corinthians 13:4-8
New International Version
4 Love is patient, love is kind. It does not envy, it does not boast, it is not proud. 5 It does not dishonor others, it is not self-seeking, it is not easily angered, it keeps no record of wrongs. 6 Love does not delight in evil but rejoices with the truth. 7 It always protects, always trusts, always hopes, always perseveres.

If any Christian tries to twist or deny those words, they are wrong and directly contradict what they believe to be *God's holy word.*

I would also like to make a note of the Old Testament. I don't think the old and new Testaments were ever meant to be one book. At the council of Nicea, a bunch of people got together and pulled random bits of writing originally unrelated to each other and smushed them together.

I am not a Christian anymore. But that doesn't mean I don't care about the church. I don't want it to fail. I want it to be a force for good. I believe it can become that, but arrogant, cruel people have stunted its growth.

Unfortunately, unless the people demand the resignation of the leaders who abuse their power and misrepresent Christ, the church will never be its best. It will be a dangerous place.

I believe there are some genuinely good people in the church. So step up and be the person you believe God has called you to be; courageous, kind, loving, and a shining example of LOVE. Stand up to the people who do harm in the church. Be brave. Be like Jesus.

Mark 11:15-17

Matthew 21:12

John 2:13-16

To people who have been hurt by the church,

It's not you. It's them. You're not broken. You're not unworthy. You are capable. You deserve to be treated with dignity and respect.

You're not perfect. That's okay. You're human. You are allowed to fail. Failure is essential for growth. It's a learning tool. It doesn't mean you deserve to go to hell.

It's good to be nice to yourself and love yourself. It doesn't mean you're arrogant.

You are enough. You are worthy with or without God.

Part 1

Prologue

He was going insane. Sam lay in bed, glaring across the room at the two people who claimed to be on his side. He wished they could understand his pain.

The small stone house was chilly, but Sam was sweating under the piles of blankets they had put on him. His blond hair was plastered against the back of his neck, and he was frustrated by the itch of the woolen tunic; he'd been wearing it for five days straight. Though his ice-blue eyes blazed with fury, he had no power to do anything.

"He keeps getting worse," Cora choked, nervously winding and unwinding a strand of blond hair around her finger.

"How much do you think he understands?" Warren questioned, holding his leather-bound Bible to his chest.

All of it, you knobheads! I'm still Sam! he tried to say, but all that came out was: "Uhl! Knohea! Thill than!"

Cora cast a worried glance at the man on the bed. "He's still Sam," she said.

I know, but you seem to have forgotten. Sam wanted to say, but all that came out was mumbled gibberish.

Warren and Cora turned away and spoke in low voices. Sam grunted, annoyed. *Look at me! Talk to me! I'm still here!* Sam tried to beg.

"I think we should send for a priest," Warren said, running his fingers along the edges of the yellowing paper.

No!

"You know he wouldn't want that," Cora said, brushing her hair behind her.

Thank you!

"God can heal all things," Warren stated, ignoring Sam. He gripped his Bible tightly as he spoke.

"Then why did he let Sam get sick in the first place?" she fired back.

Warren recoiled at her harsh tone. "God is love," he said firmly.

Cora took a calming breath and fidgeted with her hair. "I'm sorry," she said. "I know your faith means a lot to you."

Warren straightened and looked down at Cora. "The Bible says God loves everyone." he lectured. Warren looked at Sam lying helplessly in bed. *Why isn't He answering my prayers?* Warren thought, looking at the heavy book in his hands. He bit his lip nervously. *What if he dies before he comes to Jesus?* The thought of Sam and Cora going to hell made him nauseous. *I have to have faith and keep loving them as God would want.*

"I know you care about us," Cora said, pulling Warren from his thoughts. She put a comforting hand on his arm. "We appreciate everything you have done, but we just don't believe in God, especially after what happened."

"Why not?" Warren snapped.

Cora withdrew her hand and clenched her jaw. "Because belief in God is what killed our mothers," she said, gesturing to Sam. "Lord Holward had our mothers burned alive! He is one of the most ruthless and powerful people we know of, and he says *everything* he does is for God!"

"But that's not of God!" Warren insisted. "It says in the Bible to love others because God loves us."

Cora massaged her temples, blocking out Warren's voice. "No one believes that. The church says non-believers should be killed and sent to hell. Just ask Lord Holward."

Stop fighting! Sam tried to say. "Stu ightin!"

They paused and looked at Sam. "Let's go into the other room so he can sleep," Cora said.

Warren nodded in agreement.

What? No! I'm not tired! Talk to me! But as he tried to speak around his uncooperative tongue, his head spun from exhaustion. A tear rolled down his face onto the sweat-soaked pillow. Communicating would not be an option.

His soul strained against the confines of his body, but it was no use. It was making him tired.

Tears sprang to his eyes as he heard the door gently close.

Sam laid there angrily glaring at the ceiling while silent tears rolled onto the pillow.

Chapter One

Cora shivered in the damp cell.

"They're going to be okay," she told herself as tears fell down her face. Talking made the space feel less empty. "Warren took a job on that farm, and Sam is getting better."

But he wasn't getting better. Cora buried her face in her hands. Sharp pangs stabbed in her chest as she wept. "I'm so stupid!"

Her bony shoulders shook. She brushed her long, honey-colored hair from her face and rested her head against the stone wall. "The next time I see the sun will be the last," she uttered. "I hope it's a nice day."

She took out the blue wooden spinning top in her pocket and spun it. The clattering it made against the stone floor comforted her.

She got it from Sam and Warren for her 19th birthday. Sam had carved it from a block of wood, and Warren had painted it.

She smiled sadly as she remembered the day. They had gone into town and bought some sweets, then went home and spent the day playing ring toss.

She was brought out of her memories as the door opened, and a dark silhouette descended the steps. A man approached the bars and placed a torch in the sconce on the wall. He had copper curls to his brow, broad shoulders, and pale skin.

She froze when she saw his eyes. They were blood red, making him look like a demonic spirit in the torchlight. Cora was thankful for the thick metal bars between them.

"What are you?" Cora stammered, getting to her feet.

An amused smile twitched on his lips. "Hello to you too," he said in a husky Irish accent.

"What are you?" she asked again, pressing herself against the back wall.

The man chuckled. "You're the girl who angered Lord Holward," he said, eyeing her.

"It wasn't that hard," she replied. "Who and what are you?"

"My name's Ronan. Tell me what happened between you and Lord Holward," he said smoothly.

She stayed quiet as she tried to form words. Piecing it together in a coherent narrative was difficult given her scattered thoughts. "Our friend, Warren, and I were taking a trip to town with my brother, Sam," She began. "He's been sick. Some weeks he's bedridden, unable to speak, but other days, he can walk and even say a few words. We thought it would be nice to get out a bit. Sometimes Sam gets a little confused, and he bumped into Lord Holward." She paused to gather her thoughts. "Lord Holward began screaming and raised his hand to hit Sam, so I ran in front and pushed him away."

Ronan raised his brows, and his eyes widened."You're tellin' me you put your hands on Lord Holward?" he emphasized.

Cora nodded. "He said I was foolish and that I'm going to die tomorrow," she said as if it were a matter of fact.

Ronan took a moment to wrap his head around what she had said. No one in their right mind touched a Holward like that. And she spoke of her death so casually. Humans weren't known for going gracefully to their death.

"Ain't that typical. People like him can get away with doin' terrible things, but when we slightly inconvenience them, our life is on the line!" Ronan ranted.

"It's disgusting," she said bitterly. The tiny bit of cordial conversation put her slightly at ease.

Ronan took a calming breath. "What's your name?" he asked.

"Cora."

"Cora, I've come to offer you a job," he said stiffly.

"A what?" she asked, going tense again.

"Standin' up to a Holward like that is quite impressive," he continued.

"Thanks," she muttered.

"You have two choices. Either come with me, or you can go have your head cut off in the town square tomorrow."

She eyed him suspiciously. Her stomach was in knots, but her curiosity won over her apprehension. "What's the job?" she asked, moving closer to the bars.

Ronan paused as he tried to think of how to word it. "I'm a vampire," he said bluntly, giving her a fanged smile.

A small gasp escaped as her hand flew to her mouth. She took a few quick steps back as her heart thundered in her chest.

He retracted his fangs. "Just listen. I'm not goin' to hurt you," he said in a gentler tone.

She nervously fidgeted with her hair and nodded.

"The humans and vampires have an alliance. Only a handful of nobles are aware of this. Lord Nightwood allows us to stay at his castle in return for protection. We are at war with the werewolves. We're always lookin' for recruits to help out," Ronan explained.

"Werewolves?" she asked, arching a brow.

He nodded and showed his fangs again.

She went quiet, thinking. *This is crazy. But maybe I could make it work in my favor.* She confidently strode to the bars. "I'll only go with you if you help Sam," she said firmly.

Ronan smiled, extending his fangs again as he leaned on the bars. "Are you tryin' to negotiate with me? You're not in a position to do that."

She forced herself to stand her ground and meet his terrifying gaze. "If you want me that bad, you're going to help my brother. If I'm not worth that to you, then I'll gladly die."

Ronan arched his brow, impressed at her boldness. He looked down as he mulled this over. *Not only has she stood up to Lord Holward, but now she's giving* me *an ultimatum.* "Alright. If you come with me, I will do my best for your brother, and in return, you will be turned and fight alongside us."

"Deal," she said quickly before she could chicken out.

Ronan grinned. "You'll be out of here soon," he said, leaving.

***

As Ronan made his way through the maze of hallways, he passed a young woman with long brown hair. She was wearing a plain grey dress and carrying a small boy, who could have been no older than two. He was wrapped in a purple blanket. His head rested on her shoulder, sleeping peacefully.

The woman met Ronan's gaze and held the boy protectively against her. His eyes slowly inched open, and he gave a slight wave to Ronan before fluttering closed again.

"Come on, Quinn," the woman muttered, glancing nervously at Ronan as she hurried away.

"Lucky little shit," Ronan grumbled, looking around the elegant castle.

Quick footsteps echoed down the hall, coming towards him. "Ronan!" Lord Nightwood barked, approaching him.

"Yes?"

"Holward has agreed to let us take her. Now let's go before he sobers up."

Ronan chuckled. "You got him drunk?"

"Perhaps," Lord Nightwood said dismissively. "The carriage is waiting for you outside. I'll start on my way."

"Alright," Ronan replied.

He made his way back to the dungeon. A guard with a large metal key was waiting for him.

Ronan paused at the top of the steps, looking at the girl curled up in the corner of the cell. He could clearly see her bones pressing against her skin. *When was the last time she ate?* He wondered.

There was a loud metal clunk as the guard opened the cell door. She slowly sat up.

Ronan appeared in the cell and offered his hand to help her to her feet. She looked at him apprehensively. He frowned. Her eyes were so pretty, but their minty green color would soon be replaced with bright red.

16

"Come on then," he said, helping her up.

Her skin was ice cold. Ronan shrugged off his cloak and draped it over her shoulders. She froze, caught off guard at the kind gesture. "Thank you," she said slowly.

A few tears glistened in her eyes as she shook, terrified.

Ronan kept a firm arm around her as he led her out to a windowless carriage. A servant opened the door. Cora hesitated, but Ronan gently guided her in.

"You're goin' to be turned into a vampire, and you are goin' to fight against the werewolves with us," Ronan stated, getting in after her.

"What did the werewolves do?" she asked, nervously fidgeting with the ends of her hair. "Why are you fighting?"

"They're tryin' to take control of the humans and, consequently, our blood supply."

She reached into her pocket, but the top wasn't there. She checked her other pocket and felt around on the seat. It was gone.

"Lookin' for somethin'?" Ronan asked.

She sighed and shook her head. She couldn't go back for it anyway.

She had to keep asking questions to keep her mind occupied. "Why do they want to control humans?"

"The wolves believe they are the alpha species, and if they are in charge, they will bring about order. We believe that there is one high alpha at the moment who wants to rule the world, driving this current aggression by the wolves," Ronan explained.

She laughed and gently ran her hand through her hair, untangling a knot that had begun to form. "I have a difficult time believing that's what they really want," she said, smoothing her hair.

Ronan smiled. She understood. "Greedy, power-hungry bastards."

"They sound like Lord Holward," she remarked with a wry smile.

Ronan sputtered, laughing. "Very true."

"Do vampires have a leader?"

"Not really. We mostly keep each other in line. We all have a common goal, so there's rarely dissent."

"I see," Cora said slowly.

"This also means you will kill people," Ronan added.

Cora paused, letting the words sink in. "You mean werewolves?" she asked.

"Nope. Humans," he replied. "It's how you'll eat."

"What?" she gasped.

"You will be killing humans to drink their blood," Ronan repeated slowly.

Every muscle in her body was rigid. It was as if she had been turned to stone. Her mind went numb as she struggled to form thoughts. "Have you killed anyone?" she managed to ask.

Ronan nodded. "It's part of our lifestyle. It does take a bit of gettin' used to."

"Killing innocent people?" she enunciated.

Ronan shrugged. "Humans die one way or another. Doesn't matter much how."

"How can you justify something like that?" She snapped.

Ronan shrugged again. "We don't. There is no excuse for the things I've done, and there will be no excuse for the things you will do. But we come to accept it."

"Can't you try to find a better way?" she implored.

Ronan stared at her, confused. "Why would we? It would get us nowhere. Besides, we're no worse than humans."

"I don't think so," Cora snorted.

"Oh?" He laughed. "Humans kill each other all the time over weird things like war, money, sex, and power. This isn't anythin' new."

She went quiet, letting her shoulders sag as she slumped against the seats. *He's not wrong,* she realized. She hunched over and buried her head in her hands, trying to breathe deeply.

Ronan waited patiently as she processed this.

"But what would that make us? Monsters?" she asked, looking up.

"Vampires."

Chapter Two

Ronan led her to the servant's quarters in Lord Nightwood's castle. He opened the door to a small bedroom and pulled her in.

"What are we doing here?" she stammered.

A large man with short messy brown hair, a round face, and red eyes lounged on the bed, lazily plucking a happy tune on a harp made of bone.

He stopped playing and arched a brow as his gaze settled on Cora. The vampire got up and lumbered over to them. He stood a few inches taller than Ronan. He looked at her with predatory, hungry eyes.

"Is this the best you could do, Ronan? She's so small we wouldn't get much out of her," the man said in a husky voice.

Cora tried to take a few steps back, but Ronan grabbed her arm, jerking her back in place. Tears blurred her vision as she shook, terrified.

"For your information Max, she's goin' to be fightin' with us," Ronan stated.

Max threw his head back, laughing. "This little thing?"

A slight smile twitched on Ronan's lips. "I took her because she stood up to Lord Holward," he said smoothly.

Max immediately stopped laughing, bewildered. The name "Holward" was *never* spoken lightly. *"Her?"* he pointed to Cora. "This- this little girl stood up to a Holward? How?"

Ronan nodded in her direction. "Tell him."

"He was going to hurt my brother, so I pushed him," she mumbled, looking down.

Max's eyes widened, and his brows raised in shock. "Are you serious?"

"I found her in his dungeon. She was goin' to be executed tomorrow," Ronan explained.

"Oh my. I'm so sorry, miss. What's your name if you don't mind?" he stammered quickly.

"Cora," she replied quietly.

"Cora. I apologize for my rudeness," he said, dipping his head respectfully.

She didn't respond. The drastic change in tone put her more on edge. She tried to step back again, but Ronan kept a firm grip on her.

"So are ya gonna stand there, or are you goin' to let us in?" Ronan said impatiently.

Max blinked as if coming back to the present and nodded. "Cora, I am so sorry this has happened to you. If you need anything, please feel free to ask," he said, gripping the bottom of the bed and lifting it.

A panel that led to a spiral staircase opened. Ronan gave a polite nod to Max as he led her down to a large room. Crimson tapestries were draped on the wall.

Large white chandeliers decorated with rubies hung from the ceiling. Cora squinted and gasped. The chandeliers were made from the skeletal remains of humans. She tried to backpedal, but Ronan still held her arm in his steely grip.

Tears blurred her vision as her chest clenched. She tried to feel around in her pockets for the top. A sob escaped when she remembered it wasn't there.

Long stone tables stretched across the room with crystal wine bottles filled with red liquid. "Th-that's blood," she stammered.

"Yes," Ronan said, drawing her close and putting an arm around her.

A few smaller tables were pushed against the walls with chess boards out. The chairs were made from bones like the chandeliers with red cushions on them.

A few people stared at her as they passed. Cora kept her eyes to the floor, trying to stay calm. She hoped they wouldn't notice her tears.

A thin vampire with shoulder-length strawberry blond hair hunched over a pile of bones they were building into a chair. "Ronan! You're back! How was the trip?" they called, giving him a toothy grin.

"Very good!" He replied. "Brought someone back."

The vampire looked at Cora skeptically and scrunched their nose. "Food or a recruit?" they asked, getting up and walking over to the two.

"Recruit," Ronan replied.

Their expression softened. "I'm so sorry this is happening," they said somberly. "If you need anything, please ask. My name's Lance."

Cora looked away and nodded mutely.

"I should get her to bed," Ronan said.

"I thought you said she's a recruit," Lance said, confused.

"She stood up to Lord Holward for her brother. She deserves a few days of rest," Ronan explained.

Lance's brows raised, surprised. "You're not serious! Lord *Holward*?"

Ronan nodded.

Lance stared at her wide-eyed as they searched for words but came up empty.

"We'll see you later," Ronan said, leading her away.

He brought her to a small bedroom. Wolfskin blankets were piled on a bed, and a leather trunk served as a nightstand. A fireplace and bucket of coal sat opposite the bed.

"Woah!" she said, looking around. "Do I get this to myself?"

Ronan smiled sadly. "Yeah. I'll have some clothes and food brought down," he said.

Cora furrowed her brow. "I thought you were going to turn me."

"We're just takin' it slow. I want you to have a few more days of bein' human. After standin' up to a Holward, you've earned it."

Cora laughed bitterly. "Thank you."

"Is there anything I can get you?" he asked.

She shook her head and went to take his cloak off, but he stopped her. "Let me make a fire for you first," he said.

"Okay," she said, carefully lowering herself onto the bed.

Ronan knelt and made a fire with a piece of flint and steel. "That should do it," Ronan said, getting to his feet.

Pleasant warmth slowly spread in the room. "Thank you," Cora said, returning the cloak to him.

Ronan gave her a polite nod, stepped out, and locked the door. She flinched, hearing the lock slide into place. "Oh god," she choked, burying her head in her hands.

She knew what she had agreed to, but she still couldn't accept it. "This can't be real!" she gasped. "Please don't let this be real!"

***

Cora flinched as the sound of a knock on her door brought her back to reality. She sat up and wiped her eyes, taking a few deep breaths. "Come in," she said.

As the door opened, the smell of beef stew wafted in. The servant placed it on the small table and left. Another servant laid a grey tunic and black pants on the bed.

They gave her a polite nod and left. Cora was stunned. She slowly got up and went to the table where the food was placed. There was even a roll of bread and a large pitcher of ale.

Cora ate, got changed, and did her best to sleep, but her thoughts wouldn't stop racing as vast waves of emotion bombarded her, keeping her wide awake.

A knock came at the door, jarring her from her thoughts. "Come in!" she called, sitting up.

"How are you holdin' up?" Ronan asked, approaching the bed.

"I want to talk about Sam now," she said quickly.

Ronan furrowed his brow and looked away. He admired her spirit and how much she loved her brother. "Alright. What's wrong with him?"

"We're not too sure, but he bleeds out fast, and he has a hard time thinking and is always tired. When Lord Holward hit him, he may have hurt him. I don't even know if he's dead." she wiped her tears with her sleeve.

"So we can't turn him," Ronan muttered to himself. "If he bleeds out too fast, we won't be able to bring him back."

Cora nervously played with her hair. "So then what do we do? I have tried every herbal remedy I can think of," Cora said sadly.

"There are some alternatives we can try out," Ronan said.

"Alternatives?" she asked slowly.

He gave her a tight smile. "How do you feel about dark magic?"

"Magic?"

Ronan nodded. "Enchantments, potions, things like that."

"I'll do anything," Cora replied.

"I'll see what I can find," he said as he stood to leave but paused. "Cora?"

"Yes?"

"What you're doin' for your brother...it's courageous."

She laughed bitterly. "Thank you."

He gave her a tight smile before locking the door behind him.

Cora exhaled as she fell back on the pillow. *At least Ronan seemed nice.*

She reached for the top again but then remembered it wasn't there. She couldn't stop herself from crying once more at its loss. Her head and chest hurt from crying. She couldn't sleep, so she allowed herself to get lost in memories of when things were happier before Sam got sick...

Chapter Three

Cora sat on her bed, trying to focus on the book of poems Ronan had given her. He said it would help keep her mind distracted.

He kept her locked in the bedroom, primarily for her safety. He wanted to make sure the other vampires wouldn't drain her.

After a few days, she began to look a little healthier. Ronan had brought her plenty of food and water, trying to keep her as comfortable as possible. Her cheeks had developed a rosy color, and her skeletal form had been replaced by one of a healthy young woman

The heavy lock clunked, and Ronan opened the door.

"Why don't I show ya around?" he suggested.

She gave him a slight smile and put the book aside as he led her out. Ronan was sure to keep her close.

He paused in front of a steel door. "This is the dungeon, where we kill and drain humans."

"Will I have to?" she stammered.

Ronan nodded. "Yes, but it is quite fun," he said, smiling as fond memories ran through his mind. "It's a wonderful way to get to know a person."

Cora's eyes went wide with horror. "You get to know them?" she uttered.

"Yes, but really we get to know each other. You can tell a lot about a person by how they kill someone."

"I don't want to kill people," she stuttered, twisting and untwisting a bit of her hair.

He put a comforting hand on her shoulder. "You'll get used to it."

"What if I don't want to get used to it?" she asked, still fidgeting.

Ronan paused and looked away. "You don't have to worry about that now. Why don't I show you the library?"

"You have a library?" she asked, perking up and brushing the hair behind her shoulder.

"Of course we do. We need somethin' to do durin' the daylight hours."

He led her to a silver door. She opened it, and they stepped out onto an indoor stone balcony with stairs on either side. It looked over a massive library. The ceiling was an intricate mosaic made from bones and gemstones. Rows of bookshelves also made from human remains lined the walls and formed a labyrinth. There was a large fireplace in the middle with blue velvet cushions to lounge on.

Vampires quietly read as they sipped blood from crystal glasses and wine bottles.

"This is amazing!" She said with a wide smile. "Do you think we'll find some answers about Sam?"

"Absolutely," he replied.

Cora and Ronan slowly made their way through the shelves grabbing books. They sat by the fire as they researched.

After a while, Ronan turned to Cora. "I may have found a way to help your brother," he said.

"Really?" she squeaked excitedly.

Ronan nodded. "It's a sleepin' potion that will freeze him. It won't cure him, but he won't get any worse. It will buy us more time to figure somethin' else out."

Cora wilted a little disappointed. "It's a step in the right direction," she said with a sad smile.

"I still have to gather a few ingredients, but makin' it should be no problem. What's Sam's favorite food?"

"Apples. He loves anything with apples, pies, pastries, you name it. Why do you ask?"

"It's easier to get them to take it if it's on a food they like," Ronan explained.

Chapter Four

Cora just finished her evening meal when Ronan knocked on the door and came in.

"It's almost dark. Why don't you come out with me? I can show you what I like to do at night." he paused. "When I'm not out huntin'. It'll do ya good to get some fresh air."

"Okay," she said flatly, setting the tray aside and getting up.

He guided her out the back entrance. She breathed in the scent of pine trees and dirt, and it helped clear her head. The cool air gently tousled her hair and reminded her she was alive, but also that she was a prisoner waiting to be turned into a monster.

Her heart clenched as a wave of anxiety blew over her. She stopped walking as her breath got caught in her chest. *I'm fine,* she lied to herself, pushing down her fear. The anxiety simmered down to a dull ache in her chest that she just barely managed to ignore.

Ronan glanced curiously at her. "Are you alright?" he asked.

"Yeah," she said, quickly looking away.

They walked to the stables and took a seat on a bale of hay.

A striped cat with a collar that said "Rexi" pranced along with another cat wearing a yellow collar that read "Bear." They confidently walked up to the water trough for the horses. Rexi leaped in, splashing Ronan.

Ronan sighed and shook his head. "Bear, don't do it," he said to the other cat, who was looking at the water trough hesitantly.

Bear carefully climbed in and joined Rexi.

"Rexi, always gettin' poor Bear into trouble," Ronan muttered.

Cora nodded mutely and looked away.

Ronan frowned as he took note of her hands clasped tightly together, trembling.

"It's okay to be scared," he said, gently reaching out to touch her hands, but she pulled away.

"Is it?" she replied bitterly.

"Of course it is," Ronan said.

Cora turned away and looked around. She didn't want to talk. Two brown cats with black stripes cautiously eyed Cora. They looked identical, but one had a crudely made blue collar, and the other had a green one. "Come here, Rosa and Edwin," he said, holding out his hand.

The cat with the green collar slowly sauntered over and let Ronan pet her. She jumped into Ronan's lap and curled up. "This is Rosa," he said.

Cora hugged her knees to her chest and didn't respond.

The one in the blue collar nearly jumped on top of Rosa. Ronan grabbed the cat, and it slowly settled down. "And this is Edwin. She's a bit of a handful," he said, cradling her like a baby.

Cora remained silent, struggling to keep her emotion tucked away.

"It would be scary for anyone," Ronan said gently, petting the cats.

"As if you would understand," Cora grumbled.

Ronan's heart sank. He held Rosa and Edwin close and buried his nose in their fur. Rosa wiggled out of his arms and trotted off, but Edwin stayed, purring content.

"I actually do," Ronan replied. "I was human once too."

She lifted her head to look at him.

"I didn't have a choice in this either," he continued.

"What happened? How did you turn?" she asked, shifting to face him.

Ronan's expression clouded over with sadness, and his shoulders slumped. "My friend, Hank, sold me out...."

The arrow pierced the deer's skull, and it went down.
"Well done," Hank said, but Ronan ignored him.

28

He got up and ran to make sure it was dead. He knelt down and pulled the arrow from the deer. "Thank you," Ronan said, putting the arrow in his quiver.

"You're welcome," Hank said, approaching him.

Ronan chuckled. "Not you. The deer."

"Oh...of course," Hank stammered.

Ronan knelt and took out a small handful of seeds and placed them on the ground, and said a quick prayer of thanks.

Hank looked around nervously. "We should get going," he said.

"Alright," Ronan sighed, bending over to pick up the corpse of the deer, but Hank stopped him.

"I'll carry it," he said, hoisting the deer into the cart.

Ronan smiled. "Thank you."

Hank smiled nervously but didn't say anything.

"And thank you for these steel arrows," Ronan continued. "They must have cost a fortune."

"You're welcome," Hank stammered.

"And I noticed the tips are silver. Truly how could you afford this?"

"I...uh...had a good day at the market yesterday. I sold a lot of bread," Hank replied.

"I've missed gettin' to hunt with you. I know you've been busy with the bakery. But I'm happy business has been good."

Hank didn't respond and kept his head down as they walked.

Ronan paused and put a hand on Hank's arm. "Are you okay?" he asked. "You've been quiet."

Before he could respond, something rustled the bushes. Ronan froze. It was big, and Hank held a blood-soaked juicy meat sack, a perfect meal for a bear or wolf.

Another rustle from the other side. There were two.

He looked at Hank, who was nearly shaking.

"Run," Ronan said in a low voice, loading an arrow just as something leaped from the bush.

Ronan fired an arrow, hitting it in the head. It looked like a person.

"Oh my god," Ronan uttered. "I've shot someone."

Before he could do anything, someone from behind him ripped the bow and arrows from his hands and pinned his arms behind his back.

Ronan tried to jerk himself free but couldn't.

"Don't hurt yourself," a low voice said in his ear.

"I told you he was good." Hank stammered.

The person he had shot got to their feet.

"What the hell?" Ronan snapped, trying to free himself again.

The person had a narrow frame and short strawberry blond hair. They pulled the arrow from their head, and the wound miraculously healed before them. "I see that," they replied. "We'll take him."

"What?" Ronan stammered and tried to twist out of the man's grip, but he couldn't. He glanced up at the man holding him. He had messy brown hair, ashen skin, and red eyes.

"What are you?" he asked, going still.

The blond one approached Ronan and studied him. They stood an inch or two shorter than him. The person broke out into a friendly smile. "I'm called Lance," they said, holding out their hand.

Ronan tried to shake his hand, but he was completely immobilized.

Lance withdrew their hand, embarrassed. "And this is Max," they said, gesturing to the man who had Ronan's arms behind his back.

Ronan looked to Hank, who was visibly trembling, still gripping the handle of the cart.

Ronan tried to pull away once more, but he was still stuck. His heart rate quickened, and he couldn't get a full breath of air in. His vision went in and out of focus as he struggled for air.

Max bent down to speak in Ronan's ear. "Breathe. It's okay. Breathe." His voice was gruff yet soothing.

Ronan choked, trying to breathe. "Come on now, Ronan, breathe in," Max said, lightly squeezing his arms.

Ronan sucked in a shaky breath.

"Now let it out," Max said, loosening his grip.

Ronan let out the breath.

Max coached him through three more deep breaths.

He leaned against Max, exhausted. The only thing that kept him from collapsing was Max still holding him in place. He blinked. Only a few moments had passed, but it felt like an eternity.

His clothes stuck to his back with sweat.

Lance sighed sympathetically and shot Hank a sharp glare. "You don't feel bad about this?" they asked, gesturing to Ronan.

Hank looked away, ashamed. "I-I should get home," he stammered.

Lance laughed and blocked his path. "This is why we have no respect for humans. You sell each other out so easily." he sneered.

"It wasn't easy." Hank protested.

"We would never do anything like this to Ronan once he's changed," Max commented.

"What are you talkin' about?" Ronan sputtered.

Max looked at him sympathetically. "Your friend here sold you out."

"What?" Ronan uttered.

"They were going to kill me!" Hank sputtered. "They needed someone good with a bow. What was I supposed to do?"

Ronan froze, shocked. He bit his lip and looked away as a few tears fell as shame rushed through him. "I thought we were friends," he forced out.

Lance and Max sighed sympathetically as they glared at Hank.

"Ronan, I'm so sorry. Please try to understand!" Hank begged.

Ronan laughed bitterly. "Wow. You really don't know me to do you?"

"We've been friends for years. Of course, I know you." Hank insisted.

"Shut up!" Ronan snapped, fury blazing in his eyes. "If you had told me about this, I would have done it in a heartbeat for you."

Lance and Max sighed again.

Hank shifted uncomfortably. "Why are you looking at me like that? I did what I had to. You were the ones who forced me into this."

Lance rolled their eyes. "We didn't force you into this. We exploited your disloyalty and cowardice for our own gain."

"You sold out your friend to us; there's no justification. Especially since he would have done this voluntarily. You're a coward," Max laughed.

Ronan looked at Max, confused. This didn't make sense.

Max gave Ronan a kind smile, putting him a bit at ease. "We're not going to hurt you. It's going to be okay."

"Let's get him out of here," Lance said.

Ronan glared at Hank through his tears as they dragged him away. "I don't forgive you," he said bluntly.

"...When I woke up, I was here. Bein' turned like that was one of the most terrifying experiences of my life." His voice was strained as he talked.

He paused, taking a moment to compose himself. "The worst part was this man was like a brother to me. We became friends rather quickly, and he was the one person who I could count on. If I needed my bow fixed, he would get it done. If I needed more arrows, he would buy me a dozen. He even comforted me after my mother died. I felt safe with him."

"That's awful," she said sympathetically.

He shrugged. "It turned out alright, I suppose. Everyone was very kind once I got here. At least vampires don't backstab each other."

"Really?" she asked skeptically.

He nodded. " We're all working towards the same goal. We have to stay focused. Not to mention we've all gained quite a bit of wisdom with our age. We try to take care of each other."

"I see," she said slowly. "So you have to pretend to like each other?"

Ronan laughed. "We're old enough to know not to waste our energy squabbling. It's exhausting."

"So you recruit people by kidnapping them and then forcing them to fight?" she asked.

Ronan shrugged. "Once they're turned, it's pretty easy to win them over, so they want to fight with us."

"How?"

"We treat them better than humans have treated them. Sadly that's not hard to do. You would be shocked how easy it is to win a person's loyalty if you treat them well," Ronan said. "And of course, there are many other ways of gettin' people to do what you want. Fear and shame are two. But we all have a deep respect and gratitude for those who willingly or unwillingly fight for us. It's not trivial, and we've all been there. So we know how to help em' adjust."

Cora looked away, letting her thoughts wander.

"So tell me more about Sam and Warren," Ronan said.

"Warren isn't our brother by blood. Sam and I are half-siblings. We had the same father and different mothers."

"Really?"

"Yeah. Our mothers were lovers."

"Pardon?" he sputtered.

"They were lovers. They wanted children, so they slept with a clergyman. We never knew him. Our mothers were strange. They talked to nature as if it would talk back, and they swore it did," she said, with a sad smile.

"They sound like lovely people," Ronan said.

"They were." She paused to swallow a lump in her throat. "When we were 12, our mothers were burned at the stake, accused of devil worship. A priest dragged Sam and me from our home before we could see..." Her voice caught in her throat as a sob escaped.

Ronan held her close, unsure what to say, so he stayed quiet.

"The priest took us to a monastery where we met Warren," she hiccuped. "He always tried to do the right thing. *Always*. He had a different interpretation of the Bible than most."

"In what way?"

"Warren was convinced it said to love everyone." she laughed through her tears.

Ronan snorted. "Wow."

" Warren tried to love us because he thought that it would make us believe in god."

"Did it work?" Ronan mentally kicked himself. The question seemed so stupid.

She smiled sadly. "No, but Warren became like another sibling to us." she paused as her face fell. "Sam got caught stealing from the offerings. He wanted to buy apple tarts because they were in season. And the clergymen beat him within an inch of his life. Then the priests kicked us out that night."

"What about Warren?"

"He opted to come with us. He was still determined to love us out of our sinful ways. He grew colder as time went on. I think he realized he did everything for nothing. We were never going to truly repent. Not after the church killed our mothers." she paused. "Lord Holward gave the order to have the land and people 'cleansed' because the king was coming to visit."

She wiped her eyes on her sleeve.

"I'm so sorry," he murmured, embracing her in a gentle hug.

Her heart skipped a beat at his cool touch. "Thank you," she said, relaxing in his arms.

A large grey dog with short hair and floppy ears bounded up to Ronan, tail whipping back and forth furiously. Ronan bent down and pet him."This here's Bruce," he said.

Bruce swiped his huge slobbery tongue across Ronan's face before looking at Cora curiously.

"Pah!" Ronan wiped the spit off his face with his cloak.

Bruce shook his head, whipping Cora with his ears and flinging a glob of saliva into her hair.

Cora giggled and sat down to pet Bruce. He happily nuzzled into her.

Bruce laid down and rested his head on Cora's lap.

Another striped cat ran up to Ronan and began nibbling on his boot. "Hey, now Chili! Stop that," he chided, yanking his foot free.

Rosa jumped out of his lap and ran off.

Ronan pulled out a small piece of string and dangled it in front of Chili. He batted it frantically with his paws. Ronan chuckled.

Cora eyed him carefully as she absentmindedly pet Bruce, who was fast asleep. "I wouldn't have expected this from someone like you," she commented.

"What's that supposed to mean?" he asked playfully.

Chili yanked the toy from Ronan's hand and ran off.

"You...kill humans, and here you are playing with animals?" she said hesitantly, hoping she wasn't rude.

Ronan shrugged. "I've always liked animals more than humans, even before I was turned."

"Would it be okay to ask what happened...and how you got here?"

He smiled sadly and let out a long sigh. "I suppose I could tell you. I grew up in Ireland, but after my father died, my mother and I came here to work as a servant for Lord Gerwald. He didn't treat us well, but we didn't have any other options."

"Nobles are a bunch of entitled knobheads," she said, shaking her head.

"I know. That's why I like animals more. They're simple. They don't have all these complicated rules. There's no betraying the ones they care for," Ronan said.

A well-groomed brown and white dog with long wispy hair with a red ribbon tied around his neck pranced up to Ronan and gave him a playful nudge.

"Moe!" Ronan said, petting the dog. "Haven't seen you around here. Is that spoiled little girl tormenting you?"

Moe's entire backside wiggled in excitement.

"What girl?" Cora asked.

"Lord Nightwood and his wife had a little girl. This precious boy was a gift for the little lady," Ronan explained. "This is why humans make me so angry. Down here, Moe's just another one of the dogs. He's not Lady Marie's prized pet; he's just Moe. Simple."

Moe's tongue lolled out the side as she scratched him behind the ear.

"He likes you. You're very good with animals," Ronan commented.

"My mother would bring home injured animals. Guess who was her number one assistant?" She paused as her smile faded at the mention of her mother. "How do you get tired? I thought you didn't sleep," she asked.

"We still get emotionally drained. That's why so many of us read books or have hobbies. It gives us a way to recharge without sleeping."

She looked away as she tried to picture what it would be like not to sleep. "That sounds awful," she said nervously.

"It's not that bad when you get used to it. Feeding animals is my way of unwinding. It makes me happy."

Bruce woke up and trotted around to Ronan's other side. He nudged him with his nose and let out a deep *rooooo!*

"Oh, don't give me that." Ronan chided.

Bruce cocked his head to the side.

Ronan got up and helped Cora to her feet, and walked over to an entire bowl of food. "You have food! Eat it!" he said, exasperated.

Bruce sat and licked his chops, keeping his gaze on Ronan and away from his food. A brown and black striped cat and sat next to Bruce and mewled longingly.

"Not you too, Astrix. It's right there!" Ronan emphasized, gesturing to the bowl.

They blinked, keeping their eyes off the food. He let out a long sigh and hung his head. "Alright. Come on."

He led them into the mostly empty kitchen. Only a few servants were up, cleaning. Ronan carefully guided Cora over to a large rack of salted meat drying. He made sure none of the servants were looking and quickly swiped two pieces of meat. "You saw nothin'," Ronan whispered to Cora.

She smiled. "Saw what?"

He chuckled and rolled his eyes and walked back to the food bowl, and dropped the meat in. Bruce and Asrix eagerly gobbled down the meat.

"You two are almost as spoiled as Moe." Ronan laughed.

"Moe is treated differently?" Cora asked.

"Of course he is. He's Marie's pup," he replied.

"I see," Cora said, nodding.

Silence filled the empty space as she let her thoughts wander.

"Do the servants know what you are?" she asked, slicing through the quiet.

"They know not to ask questions, and they won't be hurt," he replied.

Cora looked away nervously. "You said you did archery?" She stammered, changing the topic.

Ronan nodded. "I was a hunter."

Cora looked from the animals happily eating to Ronan. "You do seem to love animals," she commented.

"Yeah. My father was a hunter. That's actually where I got my love of animals. They're so fascinatin', and I loved just watching 'em.' I made sure to get really good, so I could kill em' in one shot, and they wouldn't suffer."

"So you're pretty good with a bow then?"

"Yes," he said bluntly.

"Can I see?"

"Sure."

***

Cora tossed the rotten apple in the air. Ronan pulled the string back and released it. The arrow easily punctured the fruit and slammed into a small tree, knocking it over.

"Whoa!" Cora squealed. "That was amazing."

They walked to the tree. It was lying on the ground, nearly splintered in half.

"I used a vampiric bow," he said proudly, showing her.

"Is that different from a regular bow?"

He nodded. "It's made of steel. The arrows are tin with silver tips and raven feathers."

"Wow…" she said, carefully taking the bow. It looked so sleek and elegant.

"We should get inside," he said. "Sunrise isn't far off."

As they made their way back inside, Ronan told her more about being a vampire.

"Don't ever let a wolf get too close to ya. Their bite is poison to us, and they are much stronger, so if they get their paws on you, it's all over."

"And I'm supposed to fight these things?" she sputtered.

"We're faster, so it's pretty easy to outrun em'." he paused. "If a wolf does manage to bite you, there is a small chance of survival if you manage to kill and drain it. Then you will become a Vayer."

"A what?"

"You'll be able to walk in the daylight if you are properly covered; you'll be a bit slower than a vampire but not by much and a bit stronger. You'll also be able to steal the soul of a human."

"Really?" she asked, leaning forward.

"I've read that vayers and werewolves can take a soul on the full moon. The human would then be bound to them. They won't die unless the Vayer or wolf dies."

Cora's eyes lit up. "We could do that for Sam!"

"No," Ronan said bluntly. "That is far too risky. Out of the question."

Cora sighed and grumbled in a reluctant agreement.

Chapter Five

The next night they planned to go out again. They opened the door, and it was pouring rain. Ronan frowned. "Aw, bad luck."

Cora's face lit up as she ran out into the rain. She laughed as she splashed in a puddle.

Ronan hesitantly followed. Her smile was so pure and genuine. Ronan grinned too. "You like the rain?" He asked.

"Of course I do," she said, spinning.

"You don't find it gloomy?"

She stopped and faced him. "No, it's healing."

A clap of thunder cracked across the sky.

"Really? You don't find it frightening?" Ronan asked, shrinking back.

Cora laughed. "Healing? Well, sure, of course, healing is frightening, but it's worth it."

He stared at her blankly. "I meant the storm."

"Oh. It's a bit scary, I suppose," she said dismissively.

"You really are somethin' else, Cora," he said.

"That's what I keep hearing."

Ronan began to shiver. "It's freezing. I need to get a drink."

"Wait!" Cora said, holding out her arm. "I haven't seen a good rainstorm in a long time."

Ronan looked at her outstretched arm, confused. "I don't understand."

"You can have some of my blood. It's going to be drained at some point. Right?"

"Well, yes, but I won't be turnin' you tonight," he stammered.

"That's fine. Come on, I want to stay outside," she begged. "Please!"

A flash of lightning splintered across the sky. "It's so beautiful!" she squealed excitedly. "Please!"

He recoiled and stepped back. She was crazy. "Cora, offering your blood to me-you have no idea what that means, do you? I am a vampire, a human's most dangerous predator. I could drain you here and now if I wanted to. I could destroy you. I could kill you. For someone to willingly allow a vampire to drink from them is. That's- that's a gift I do not deserve." he said, getting choked up.

"I trust you," she said. "Please!"

Ronan shivered as he looked at the succulent veins running beneath her skin. He walked over to her and pulled her in for a hug. "Thank you," he said.

They sat on a tree stump. Ronan tilted her head to the side. "It will be easier to hold still like this. It will hurt if you move too much."

"Okay," she said.

He pulled her close and looked into her eyes. Every muscle in her body relaxed as a peaceful calm came over her. He wound his arm around her and took her wrist in his other hand, finding her pulse. He carefully bit into her neck. She winced at the sharp pain. The rain falling against her skin was a good distraction from the pain.

She watched the lighting overhead as he drank, feeling happier than she had in a while.

The warmth rushed into him as he kept careful tabs on her pulse so he wouldn't take too much.

He pulled back, discreetly wiping the blood from his lips on his cloak.

"So, how was it?" she asked.

Roman laughed. "Very good. Are you okay?"

She nodded. "Let's go for a walk."

"Okay."

He helped her to her feet, and they walked along the castle wall. Going into the woods would be too dangerous during a thunderstorm.

"So, how did you come to like the rain?" Ronan asked as they walked.

"Mother Martha, my mother, liked to dance with nature. She danced with the rain, wind, water, trees. Mother Grace, Sam, and I would sit outside and watch the lightning wrapped in a big blanket we all made." She smiled sadly.

"Your family sounds wonderful."

She nodded quietly. Her face brightened when she saw a particularly deep puddle. She ran and jumped in it, splashing Ronan. "Hey there." he laughed, kicking the puddle spraying her back.

Her stomach howled. "We should get inside," Ronan said.

"Alright." She took a step, but her foot slipped from under her. Ronan scooped her up in his arms before she fell.

"Is this necessary?" she complained as he carried her inside.

"I need to keep you in one piece," he replied with a slight smile.

When they got inside, he paused a moment more, savoring the feeling of her body against his before setting her down by the fire in the servant's hall.

"I'll get somethin' for you to eat," he said.

She went to sit on a chair, but Ronan quickly swept her aside and picked up a lizard that had climbed on it. "What are you doin' down here? You should be by the pond," he chided.

Cora furrowed her brow, confused.

"Oh, How rude of me," Ronan said, holding up the lizard. "This is Elizabeth. I call her Ella for short."

Cora laughed. "Pleasure to make your acquaintance," she said.

Ronan smiled and put Ella back outside. He quietly slipped to the kitchen and filled a small sack with bread, cheese, and fruit for her.

"Sorry about that," he said, giving her the sack.

She took it and smiled, grateful.

He helped her up, and they went down to his room so she could eat and rest.

Chapter Six

"I'd like to show you the dungeon today," Ronan said slowly. He had come in that morning, shortly after breakfast.

Cora paused and swallowed her food. "Okay." She set her tray aside and went with him.

"It won't be pretty, but this is going to make it easier after I turn you," Ronan said slowly.

Cora nervously bit the inside of her lip; his words settled in the air. She fought back the tears, not wanting to look weak. *I can do this,* she told herself.

He put a comforting arm around her. She stayed stiff, her mind flooded with racing thoughts. This is happening. I'm going to become a murderer. A monster!

She had a fleeting moment where she wondered if this was all worth it. If even Sam was worth it. She could refuse, or if they turned her, she could get killed by a wolf. *What am I thinking? Of course, Sam is worth it.*

"You're goin' to be turned into a predator. Humans will be your life source. It's no different than a mountain lion killin' a deer," he continued.

His words became muffled as her head throbbed and her heart began to race. Don't break down. Don't break down. Don't…

She clenched her hands and collapsed in Ronan's arms, tears spilling over.

Ronan sighed sympathetically and held her as she cried. "It gets easier. I promise. We'll take it slowly," he said.

Two vampires passing by paused, seeing a human being comforted.

"Ronan," the vampire with short blond hair and scruffy beard said.

He looked up, keeping Cora close. She didn't even register the other vampire's presence.

"Yes?" Ronan said politely.

"Is that food, or is she joining us?" he asked, gesturing to Cora.

"She'll be joinin' us," Ronan responded.

The other vampire looked at her sympathetically. "I'm so sorry this is happening to you," she said gently, placing a hand on her shoulder.

Cora flinched and turned to look at her. She had long auburn hair tied back and a thin frame. "What?" Cora stammered.

The woman repeated her condolences.

"Why? Why does everyone keep saying that? No one is going to do anything to stop this! Why is everyone so sorry?" she ranted.

Ronan blinked away a few tears as he held her tight. He wished he could let her go.

The vampire sat next to her. "We've all been where you have. Being dragged into this isn't easy," she said.

Cora relaxed slightly in his arms.

"Today is going to be her first," Ronan said.

The vampire with short hair shook his head sadly. "What's your name?" he asked gently.

"Cora," she responded, wiping away a tear.

"I'm Mark, and this is my sister, Willow," he said, gesturing to the vampire next to him.

Willow gave a small wave.

Mark shifted his weight and looked up, getting lost in thought. "I remember my first kill. I cried for days after." He paused, face falling. "Of course, that was after I was turned." He shuddered.

"I think I cried a week straight," Willow added.

"Don't you ever feel bad about what you do?" Cora questioned.

The three vampires laughed as though she had just asked a stupid question. Cora shrank back, embarrassed.

"No," Mark scoffed.

"But these are *people*," Cora protested.

"They're going to die one way or the other. At least when we kill them, we use them for sustenance," Willow explained patiently.

Not one trace of guilt could be found among them. They were happy. Cora relaxed and leaned into Ronan.

"I promise it will be okay," Ronan said.

Cora nodded mutely. "Let's get this over with," she said.

"We'll clean up so you can be with Cora," Mark offered, turning to Ronan.

Ronan smiled gratefully and nodded. "That would be great," he said, helping Cora to her feet.

Ronan slowly opened the door. Willow gave her shoulder a comforting squeeze as they all entered.

The stench of blood and death hung heavily in the air, making Cora gag. Humans and corpses were hung on walls and locked in cages.

Cora's stomach churned as she surveyed the gruesome scene. She instinctively reached for the blue spinning top she would keep in her pocket, but of course, it wasn't there.

"Remember, they're going to die one way or another," Ronan said, putting a comforting hand on her shoulder.

Cora nodded mutely, trying to keep her lower lip from quivering. "I want to get it over with," she stammered.

Ronan guided her to a smaller cage with one person. It was an older man with greying hair, a disheveled beard, and sagging skin. "This is Lord Fadwall."

Cora's eyes widened. "What? You kill nobles?"

"We're not normally allowed to spill the blood of a noble, but the king specifically requested he is killed." Ronan smiled.

"Why?" Cora asked.

"He was planning a coup. He doesn't support the treaty," Ronan explained.

"Treaty?"

"We protect the higher-ups from werewolves, and in return, we can have our picks of the lower classes," Ronan said.

"That's horrible!"

"It is, but at least we can go after their bastards. Some of em' are as spoiled as the nobles," Ronan spat.

Willow and Mark shifted uncomfortably.

"Is he the one I have to kill?" Cora asked, glancing at the man.

"If you would like," Ronan replied gently.

Cora bit her lip as waves of nervousness rushed through her.

"O-okay," she stammered. Her legs were visibly shaking.

Ronan opened the door and chained Lord Fadwall to the wall by his wrists. He hung limp, keeping his eyes to the floor.

Cora's mind went numb as she stepped into the cell. "How do I do this?" she asked.

Ronan handed her a knife. She dropped it because her hand was shaking uncontrollably.

"Cora, this man was a close friend of Lord Holward's," Ronan said, picking up the knife.

"Really?" she asked.

"Yes," he said gently, placing it in her hand.

She gripped it tight, trying not to drop it again. "Where do I do it?" she asked hesitantly.

He spun her to face the man chained to the wall. "He was always so supportive of Lord Holward," Ronan said, ignoring her question.

Cora's expression darkened.

A wicked smile stretched across Ronan's face. "Did you know that Lord Holward was like a mentor to him?"

Just hearing the name Holward made her blood boil. Her hand steadied.

"He was very religious. He was known for attending the burnings Lord Holward did. He wanted to learn from the master."

Her hand tightened around the knife.

"He wanted to rid the land of us vampires because he believed us to be demons. He wanted the land cleansed," Ronan continued.

She clenched her jaw so hard her head began to throb. The words Lord Holward spoke as her mothers were being tied to a post ran through her head, "Heavenly Father, we commend these wicked people into your hands. Bless this fire to make it holy so that the land may be cleansed in your righteous name. Amen."

"If it were up to him, we would all be burned alive." Before Ronan could finish the sentence, Cora had driven the knife into the man's chest.

Tears streamed down her cheeks as she took out the knife and stabbed him again and again, putting all her strength into each jab. She screamed through her rage, and blood sprayed in her face.

With one final stab, every ounce of energy left her. She stopped. Her arm ached, and her throat was sore.

The gruesome scene came into focus as her mind slowly cleared.

Cora stood there stunned and shaking. The man hung limp, eyes open.

"Well done," Ronan said, gently prying the knife from her hand.

"We can clean up," Willow offered.

"Thank you," Ronan said, guiding Cora away.

She leaned on him as they walked. It felt like a part of her had been ripped out, leaving a painful gaping void.

When they got into the room, Ronan had a washbasin brought to wash off the blood.

Cora vigorously rubbed the cloth across her face as if trying to wash away what she did.

She dropped the cloth and burst out sobbing. Ronan pulled her close. "You did so well," he said soothingly.

All she could do was whimper in response.

"It's going to get better," he reassured. "Especially after you're turned."

"Tomorrow," she choked.

"What?"

"I want to be turned tomorrow. I want it to be done," she begged.

"Alright," he said gently, brushing away some hair that had fallen in her face.

"I don't want to be alone tonight," she stammered. "Please don't leave me."

"I won't," he said, lifting her off her feet and carefully putting her in the bed.

"Don't leave!" she enunciated, grabbing his hand.

Ronan tentatively slipped into the bed and took her into his arms.

"I want you to do it," she whimpered, leaning into him.

His arms tightened around her as a smile lit up his face. "Alright," Ronan said softly.

"Will it hurt?" she asked.

He gave her a reassuring smile as he chose his words carefully. "I'm gonna do my best to make it as painless as possible."

"What if I'm not good at being a vampire?" she asked, toying with her hair.

Ronan chuckled. "You still have a lot more trainin' to complete. You're not goin' anywhere near a wolf until we're all certain you're ready."

"What if…"

"Shhhh." He held her close and gently massaged her back. "You'll get there. It's going to be alright. The best thing you can do for yourself is rest."

She opened her mouth to protest, but he caught her gaze. A heavy fog blanketed her mind, and she found herself drifting off to sleep.

Part Two

A few months after she is turned...

Chapter Seven

Lance gracefully skipped from one branch to the next. They saw the glint of a campfire through the trees and silently glided to the edge of the branch, keeping out of sight. They peeked out and saw what was left of the West Woods wolfpack.

14 hulking beasts lumbered around a campsite. They were well over 7 feet tall with yellow eyes and razor-sharp claws. Their weapons were in hand, but they seemed to drag their feet, exhausted.

They quickly counted how many there were and ran back to the rest of the group.

Cora waited with Ronan and the other vampires by a small creek. She wore a black tunic and pants lined with animal fur to hide her scent. Her hair was pulled back into a neat braided bun, and she had a leather pouch on her hip that contained a cluster of silver throwing knives.

She glanced nervously at Ronan. "When will he be back?" she clumsily signed. Ronan taught her the hand gestures they used to communicate when they were out hunting wolves because they couldn't risk being heard.

"Soon," Ronan signed.

Lance returned, jumping from one of the trees and landing lightly on their feet.

"14 left," they signed. "All awake. They may be expecting us. We have to be quick."

Cora furrowed her brow, concerned. "Is that a lot?" she signed to Ronan.

"They used to have over 50 wolves," Ronan signed back. "16 of us can easily take on 14."

"Are we ready? Do we understand? Any questions?" Lance signed.

The group nodded and signed that they understood.

"Let's go!" Lance signed.

The vampires soundlessly ghosted through the forest. There was a faint wet dog smell in the air, along with the scent of burning wood.

Cora had to keep her focus, despite her nerves. Her hand shook as she gripped the silver throwing knife. The wet dog smell got stronger as they got closer. Ronan motioned for her to follow him up a tree.

She climbed up after him, and they took their positions.

Cora bit her lip nervously, seeing the size of the wolves, and glanced at Ronan.

He gave her a reassuring smile. "Are you okay?" he signed.

She managed to nod.

The other vampires got into their position. A brown wolf perked up, sniffed the air, and howled.

"Now!" Ronan called, firing an arrow through the wolf's chest.

Arrows and knives rained down on the wolves from the woods.

Cora threw a knife, hitting a wolf in the eye. It dropped dead.

I did it! She grinned.

"Good job!" Ronan said, firing off two arrows. "Keep going!"

She continued throwing knives, blocking out the sounds of dying howls and pained screams from the woods.

The tree they were in snapped as a tan wolf body slammed into it, throwing itself at their tree to knock them out of it.

Ronan grabbed Cora's hand, and they were out of harm's way before the tree hit the ground. The wolf charged through the trees at them. They darted up another tree, and Cora threw another knife, hitting the wolf in the shoulder. It howled in pain. Ronan shot an arrow through its head, and it dropped dead.

"Alright, that's it! We need to go!" Lance called, seeing the situation was getting out of hand.

Cora and Ronan ran back to the castle weaving through trees, crossing through several small streams, and avoiding roads until the walls of the keep were in sight.

They stumbled in through the servants entrance and to the bed with the hidden passage underneath. Ronan lifted the stairs, and they went down. "You did amazing!" Ronan said, lifting her off her feet in a hug.

She laughed, relieved. "Thank you."

Lance stepped onto a table. "We got most of them. It looks like there are five left. Great job!" They announced.

"Nice work!" Willow said as she passed.

Lance stepped down and ran to Cora. "You were amazing!" they said.

Max appeared next to her. "Congratulations, you've done well," he commented.

"Thank you," Cora said breathlessly.

"Ready to make that potion?" Ronan asked.

She smiled and nodded.

They went down into Ronan's room. All the ingredients were neatly laid on the table next to a large iron pot and an apple. A large bottle of blood, dried lavender, a bowl of water from a nearby stream, valerian root, and ginger.

"Blood?" she asked, picking up the vial.

Ronan nodded. "It's used to transfer the energy of the living. The herbs are to help him fall asleep, and the water is for cleansing and healing."

"Alright," she said, leaning on the table. "Let's get started."

***

Cora stared into the black liquid at her reflection. Her red eyes stood out against her blond hair and pale skin.

Ronan sprinkled a handful of crushed herbs into the bowl and gave her a curious look. "Are you okay?"

"I love my eye color," she said.

"Really?" Ronan asked, furrowing his brow.

"Red is my favorite color," she replied.

He chuckled. "I see." He paused, taking a moment to admire her.

She arched a brow. "Are you okay?" she asked, shifting uncomfortably under his focused stare.

He blinked. "Yes. It looks good on ya. Your eyes, I mean. But so do your clothes," he paused as he realized how dumb he sounded.

She stared at him with a mixture of confusion and uncomfortable amusement.

"But your hair is also nice," he continued, cringing internally.

He turned his eyes back to the potion, mentally kicking himself for sounding so stupid. *Why can't I get this right?*

"Thank you," she said with a slight smile. "You're sweet."

He laughed nervously, not sure how to respond. He leaned over and studied the liquid. "Alright, I think we're ready," he said.

He picked up the apple and dipped it into the potion. As he slowly lifted it out, it had a slight glow around it. Ronan wrapped it in a cloth and placed it in his bag.

Chapter Eight

They came to a small stone house nestled in a clearing. "Is this it?" Ronan asked.

"Yeah," Cora said, knocking on the door.

Warren answered the door quickly. As soon as he saw it was Cora, he swept her into a hug. "Oh god! I thought you were dead!" he choked between sobs.

She smiled. "Well, I'm not," she said, hugging him back. "How's Sam?"

Warren's arms tensed around her. "I'm just trying to make him comfortable," he said softly.

Warren pulled back and studied her. "You look different. What happened to you?" He took notice of her red eyes. "Your eyes!" he sputtered.

"It's a long story; we'll fill you in later," she replied.

Ronan cleared his throat. Warren started in surprise, suddenly realizing someone else was there. His gaze settled on Ronan's red eyes. "What are you?"

He stared back blankly at the human. "My name's Ronan."

"We think we can help Sam," Cora interjected.

"What? How?" Warren demanded. "And what did you do to your eyes?"

Cora bit her lip as she tried to think of how to word it. "I made a deal with Ronan," she said slowly.

"What kind of deal?" he inquired.

Cora looked down. "I'll explain after I take care of him," she said, gesturing to Sam.

Warren glanced at Sam in the bed and slowly stepped aside.

Sam's tired face lit up when he saw her. "Cowa!"

She forced herself to smile. "I brought you something," she said, taking out the apple.

Sam's eyes went wide, snapping into a trance. He tried to sit up but couldn't. Ronan came in and helped Sam to a sitting position.

Sam slowly lifted his hand, and Cora gave him the apple. He bit into it and sighed as he relaxed a bit. He took another bite, and his eyes began to close.

Cora grabbed Ronan's hand for comfort as she watched Sam's eyes flutter closed as he took the final bite. The apple fell from his hand and rolled onto the floor as he sank into the pillow. His face relaxed as the pain left him. Warren smiled sadly as he watched his brother's chest rise and fall.

"Thank you," Cora said, hugging Ronan.

"Now, explain," Warren said firmly.

Cora untangled herself from Ronan's arms and stooped to look under the bed. She hoped she would find the wood top as she felt around, but it wasn't there. She opened the bedside drawer, but it wasn't there either. "Warren, have you seen the blue top you and Sam gave me for my birthday?" she asked.

"No. Cora, I need an explanation," he begged.

She turned to face Warren. "The night Ronan took me, we made a deal."

"I was very impressed at her bravery. I figured she would be a good recruit," Ronan said.

"Recruited for what?" Warren demanded.

Cora looked away, trying to think of what to say. Her heart hammered in her chest as she looked at Warren, waiting patiently for a response.

"There is a war happening between vampires and werewolves," Ronan explained.

Warren laughed. "What?"

"I was turned into a vampire," she forced out.

"A blood-drinking demon?" Warren scoffed. "Cora, you could never become a demon. You're too good, too kind and caring. Besides, I'm not even sure if those exist."

Cora smiled sadly. She took a moment to appreciate the last moment of normal between her and Warren.

But Warren's expression quickly clouded over as he looked into her red eyes.

She slowly gave him a nervous smile, showing her fangs.

"Cora...what have you done?" Warren uttered.

"Warren, I had to, for Sam," she said quickly.

"I was the one who put her up to all of it. I presented the deal. I was the one who trained and turned her," Ronan interjected.

"Trained?" Warren snapped. "For what?"

"T-to kill people. So I can feed," Cora replied quietly.

"You kill people?" Warren emphasized.

"I have killed people," she said stiffly. "But I only kill humans for blood to drink. I fight werewolves in the war."

"You kill humans for their blood to *drink*?" Warren asked slowly.

"Yes," she replied.

"Humans. Living breathing humans," he stated coldly before turning to Ronan.

Ronan glared at him and nodded. "I didn't give her a choice in the matter," he stated.

Cora played with the end of her ponytail.

Warren sat and put his head in his hands, trying to think. *This isn't Cora. She would never hurt anyone,* Warren thought.

"Warren…" she started to say, but he immediately dropped to his knees, clasping his hands together. His knuckles were white, beads of sweat formed on his brow.

"Take me," he forced out. "Not her! God, you are good. You are fair and just. Please take this from her! I will take her punishment! Please don't let this be!"

Ronan rolled his eyes. *So dramatic,* he thought.

Cora broke down in tears seeing Warren beg for her soul. "Warren," she said, dropping to his level.

"Take me!" Warren screamed at the ceiling, ignoring her.

"Warren," she said, placing a gentle hand on his shoulder.

"Cora! Please! Please pray with me! There has to be a way to fix this. I'm sure God will provide answers if we have faith," Warren insisted, grabbing her hands.

Her lower lip trembled as she embraced him. He sobbed into her shoulder. "I can't lose you," he whimpered.

Ronan looked away as a pang of jealousy stabbed him.

"Ronan and I have to be going soon, but I'll be back to visit. I promise," she said.

"Cora, there has to be a way to fix this," Warren said desperately.

"Maybe," she said, forcing a smile.

"Why can't you get blood without killing people? You could offer them money," Warren stammered.

Ronan threw his head back, laughing. "Pay a *human* for their blood?"

Cora chuckled nervously.

"Why not?" Warren demanded, slamming his fist angrily on the table.

"We don't have to. We don't want to. That's just so needless," Ronan laughed.

"We try to give them a painless death," Cora reassured.

Warren got to his feet, eyes blazing with fury. "This is your fault! You turned her into some unholy demon!" he said, advancing on Ronan.

Ronan held his ground and extended his fangs. "Watch it, human!" he snarled.

Warren took a few steps back, and Cora put herself between them.

"Ronan, don't hurt him," she said firmly.

He slowly retracted his fangs and relaxed.

"Cora, this is insane!" Warren snapped.

"I did this for Sam. Ronan said he would help him," she enunciated.

Ronan looked away as a pang of guilt stabbed him. He knew what was happening to her wasn't fair. His heart clenched as he wished he wasn't part of it.

"He promised he would help Sam," she repeated, gesturing to Ronan.

"How?" Warren demanded, looking at Ronan. "How is this going to help?"

"The apple had a potion in it to put him into a deep sleep. He won't get any worse or better. But this means we have more time to come up with something else," Cora explained.

Warren turned his attention back to Cora. "And what if it doesn't work? What if Sam dies anyway? You've let him turn you into a monster." Warren snarled, towering over her.

Ronan bristled, seeing Warren invading her space like that. *She can handle it*, he told himself.

"Sam's sick!" she fired back.

"And you're a monster!" Warren snapped. His venomous stare turned to Ronan. Every ounce of anger boiled over, and Warren lunged for him, but Cora pushed him against the wall, keeping him out of Ronan's reach.

Ronan bared his teeth and stepped forward, hovering over Cora, and looked Warren in the eye.

Warren whimpered but stared back defiantly. He reached over to the table and picked up a small crystal vial filled with water. "In the name of Jesus, I rebuke thee!" he declared, splashing the water in Ronan's face.

Ronan recoiled, confused. "What was that for?" he demanded.

Warren stared at Ronan, waiting for the Lord to step in. The moment stretched on, but nothing happened.

Ronan slowly dried his face with his cloak. "Why did you do that?" Ronan asked again.

Cora swiped the vial and studied it. It had a gold cross emblazoned on the front of it. "Holy water?" she asked, arching a brow.

Ronan doubled over laughing. "Did he just try to baptize me?"

Cora rolled her eyes. "I think it was supposed to be an exorcism."

Warren kept his focus on Ronan. *God will make fools of them. Any minute now.*

"Where did you get this?" Cora demanded.

"I...uh... The priest visited a while back to give me counsel when I needed it. He left this behind," Warren said quickly.

Cora looked away to hide her amusement. "Warren, I don't think God is going to be much help," she snickered.

Warren gritted his teeth angrily.

"Perhaps if we drain him, his God will show up," Ronan mocked.

"Ronan, don't," Cora said firmly.

"You! You laugh at me now when all I've done has been to help you?! You're no better than your whore mother," Warren spat.

All humor was immediately wiped away. Cora's heart shattered at his words. She stepped back, taking in what he had said. She opened her mouth to speak, but the words got caught in her throat.

Warren turned away, ashamed as a knot formed in his stomach. A small sob escaped. She was still Cora. *How could I have said that?* He knew he went too far. "I'm sorry," he uttered.

Ronan watched the silent tears fall from her face as she struggled to speak.

"Breath," Ronan said calmly as he reached out and drew her to him.

She inhaled but broke down sobbing as she exhaled. Ronan shot Warren an icy stare as he held her close.

She hugged him tight as she tried to catch her breath.

Warren looked at her in Ronan's arms. He clenched his hand until his knuckles turned white and began to shake. The way she leaned into him as he comforted her... She was in the arms of a demon—a vile, filthy servant of Satan. Warren charged at Ronan and tried to knock him away from Cora. Ronan swept Cora behind him and wrapped his hand around Warren's neck, and slammed him to the ground.

Warren wheezed as he looked around, dazed. He tried to breathe, but Ronan's grip tightened.

Ronan's eyes blazed with fury as he bared his teeth. *How dare this human attempt to overpower me?* He thought.

"Do you have any idea what I could do to you?" Ronan snarled. "You stupid, foolish human!"

"Ronan," Cora said sharply.

He ignored her, grinning as he watched Warren's face begin to purple.

"Ronan, please don't hurt him!" Cora begged, grabbing his arm, trying to pull him off.

Ronan growled, frustrated, and slowly released Warren. Cora took this opportunity to drag him to his feet. She stepped between the two as Warren tried to catch his breath. He gasped, gulping down huge lungfuls of air.

"Pathetic fragile human," Ronan muttered.

"Cora, do you understand that your soul has been *damned*? You've lost everything. You gave up your eternity in heaven with me, all for someone who may as well have been dead," Warren said, struggling to get to his feet. He leaned against the table to steady himself as the room spun.

"I know what I gave up!" she snapped, advancing on him.

Warren stumbled back, falling to the floor.

She grabbed his arm and jerked him to his feet. "I'm not stupid! Sam is worth it! I love him! He's my brother!" she emphasized.

Warren couldn't form a coherent response as his heart raced, terrified. He panicked and tried to yank his arm free. She let go, making him fall to the ground again. "Please, just leave!" he begged.

Cora froze, staring at Warren cowering on the floor. "Warren, I'm sorry," she said, stepping away from him.

"Leave," Warren said firmly.

Tears sparkled in her eyes as she opened her mouth to speak. "Just go," Warren said.

Cora stayed stiffly in place, lower lip quivering.

"I'll get Sam," Ronan said gently, disappearing into the bedroom and coming out with Sam in his arms. "Let's go."

Cora sniffled, wiped away her tears, and followed Ronan out.

They walked back through the woods in silence. She felt numb as she replayed what happened in her head. Her hands were clenched in tight fists. She kept her gaze to the ground in front of her. Her head throbbed as regret coursed through her.

Lance was carefully sawing off the hand of a human lying on a large platform with holes and a tub to catch the blood underneath.

Max sat to their left, trying to drown out the man's muffled cries as he lazily plucked at a harp carved from bone.

Lance detached the hand and began peeling off the skin and muscle to get to the bone.

The man's sobbing was grinding on Max's last nerve. Max set down the harp and grabbed a large butcher knife next to Lance.

He positioned it over the man's terrified face.

"Wait!" Lance said, quickly grabbing his wrist, holding the butcher knife.

"I can't play with this going on!" Max complained.

Lance guided his hand to the base of the man's neck. "All I ask is that you cut at the neck. I need the skull intact," they explained as they lightly trailed their finger across the man's face.

He squeezed his eyes shut as tears spilled out. "Please," he tried to beg through the gag.

Lance gently smoothed their hair back and nodded to Max.

In one quick slice, he cleanly cut the man's head off.

"It's going to make a lovely chalice," Lance said.

"You always do good work," Max remarked, picking up the harp again.

Lance smiled. "Thank you."

Max went back to strumming the harp.

Cora passed by, dirt and twigs knotted in her usually well-kept hair. Ronan was carrying an unconscious man in his arms.

Lance jumped to their feet to look at who he was carrying. "He has impeccable bone structure," they commented, eyes going wide.

She drilled them with a cold stare and stepped protectively between the two. Max gave her an apologetic smile and gently pulled Lance back a few steps.

Lance sighed, disappointed. "I assume it's not for food or for materials?"

"This is her brother, Sam," Ronan explained.

"This is him?" Lance said excitedly.

Cora nodded.

"Tell me about him!" Lance blurted out. "Will I get to meet him? What's he like?"

"Give me a moment," Cora said, going to her bedroom.

She carefully laid Sam on the bed and put a blanket on him. She smoothed back his hair and gently kissed him on the forehead. "We're almost there," Cora said with a sad smile.

She left and locked the door. She took a calming breath and rested her head on the cool metal door, taking a moment to herself before returning to the group.

"Go on then, tell us," Lance said eagerly.

"Well, let's see..." she said, thoughtfully. "Sam loves anything with apples. I mean *anything*. He doesn't know how to slow down. He's either taking odd jobs or learning a new skill," she paused as a tear slid down her face.

Lance leaned in, listening intently.

"Sometimes, he would make things. One time he made a spinning top for my birthday. I lost it a while ago," she laughed bitterly.

"He sounds very nice," Max said.

"I can't wait to meet him," Lance squealed.

Chapter Nine

Cora undid her messy bun, letting her blond hair tumbled down her shoulders. The remains of a young man's blood-stained her teeth. She had to pick a tiny bit of flesh that had been lodged between her left fang and front tooth.

She sighed, content as the warmth from the blood rushed through her. As she made her way to the library, Ronan ran up to her.

"I got a little somethin' for ya," he said eagerly.

"Really?"

He nodded and held out a large leather sack. "Open it."

She slowly untied the string and looked inside. "Oh my god," she said, pulling out a red velvet hooded cloak. "This is beautiful."

"There's somethin' else in there," he said, nudging her.

She draped the cloak around her shoulders and took out a ruby necklace. "This must have cost you a fortune!" she said as her eyes lit up.

"It cost someone a fortune," he muttered.

"And who would that be?" she asked.

He gave her an impish grin. "Let's just say Lady Anne shouldn't let her ladies maids walk around at night."

She chuckled. "Thank you."

He smiled and helped her put the necklace on. "You look gorgeous," he said.

She smiled sheepishly and looked away. "Thank you," she said, sincerely.

***

Cora walked through the woods humming to herself, her red cloak flowing behind her. She carried a small wicker basket filled with honey cakes, Warren's favorite, and a few bottles of blood in case she got thirsty.

The moonlight crept through the trees, washing the ground in a spotty pale light.

As she walked, she saw a shadow move out of the corner of her eye. She paused, surveying the surroundings. A bush rustled, and she could smell a faint musty dog scent.

Werewolf.

She knew she could get away. She was fast enough. But as she started to run, a massive grey beast cut off her path. It stood on its hind legs, baring its teeth. She felt tiny in its shadow as it stood close to seven feet tall.

Cora's legs began to shake, but in an impulsive split-second decision, she extended her arm, and the wolf lunged and sunk its teeth in.

She gasped as a sharp pain splintered through her body. Cora kicked off the ground and propelled herself around the wolf, breaking her arm. She gritted her teeth, trying to ignore the pain as her mind began to fog over.

The wolf shook her off, and she slammed into a tree, narrowly missing a sharp branch.

Her vision blurred, but she forced herself to her feet. She bared her fangs. The wolf lunged, but she clumsily leaped out of the way.

The wolf snarled, and Cora hastily stumbled to the knife. Her fingers brushed the blade, but the wolf sunk its teeth into her leg and dragged her back.

Tears fell from her face as she felt her body grow cold. The wolf kept its jaw locked on her leg. With one final burst of energy, she tried to jerk her leg away. It stumbled a few steps, giving her enough room to reach the knife.

A rush of relief coursed through her as her hand gripped the cool metal handle. As the wolf snarled and opened its jaws to go in for the kill, Cora jerked to the side and drove the knife into its skull

It let out a pathetic whine as she drove it in deeper. She gritted her teeth as she fought the pain wracking her body.

She stabbed the wolf's neck and began drinking it down. It felt like acid down her throat.

She could feel the wolf weakening and her pain slowly subsided. The wolf let out a final whimper before it died.

She shuddered and collapsed on the corpse. Every ounce of her was sore. Every breath burned her lungs as the acidic taste lingered in her mouth.

She forced herself to her feet and took out the small flask filled with blood, and drank it down. It washed away the wolf's blood.

She looked at the blue scars that ran across her forearm and smiled.

***

Cora excitedly skipped into Warren's house. "Warren, look!" she said, holding out her arm.

"Cora, I can't do this," he said, slinging a bag over his shoulder.

"Can't do what?" she asked with a nervous smile.

"This. Him. You. You sold your soul to Satan! You've become a monster." He paused as a tear escaped. "I failed. I can't save you. I won't be part of this! I won't have any sort of relationship with a disciple of Satan!"

"It was never your job to save us," she protested.

"I prayed so hard for both of you. I loved you. But it hasn't done any good. You have damned yourself, and possibly Sam too."

"At least in hell, I won't be stuck with an arrogant tyrant that killed my moms." she fired back.

"Lord Holward killed them!" Warren enunciated.

"For your god!"

Warren stepped back and took a moment to clear his thoughts. "You're right. I thought Christianity was about loving others. But it doesn't work. I'm going to seminary. I can't stay here! I need to figure this out."

"No! What about me? What about Sam?"

"Not my problem." he snapped as he headed for the door.

"You don't even have the decency to wait until Sam wakes up." she fired.

Warren paused. "I know you'll take care of him," he said as he turned away.

"If you leave, you can't come back," Cora said quickly.

Warren stopped with his hand on the knob. "I know," he replied.

"Warren, please!" she begged desperately as he went out the door. "Warren!" she called again. He kept walking and didn't look back. Cora sank to the floor in tears. "We were so close!" she sobbed.

Her chest ached as she imagined a future without Warren. He was always the first to offer comfort and compassion.

I have to keep going. Cora told herself.

Chapter Ten

Cora got to the servant's entrance at the same time as Ronan. He eyed her disheveled hair and torn sleeve. "What happened?" he asked.

"I got bitten by a werewolf," she said, proudly showing him the bitemark.

Ronan recoiled as if the wound was toxic. "How?" he sputtered.

"I ran into a wolf on the way to Warren's, and it bit me. Now I can take Sam's soul," she said, excited. "Right?"

Ronan nodded mutely as he stared at the bite mark.

Cora pushed past him to go inside, and he followed her.

"Did you try to let yourself get bitten?" Ronan stammered.

"Yeah," she said slowly.

He grabbed her arm, stopping her. "Why would you do something so stupid?" Ronan snapped. "You could have been killed!"

"But I wasn't!" she said sharply, yanking her arm away. "What's done is done! I'm fine!"

Ronan bit back a scathing remark. He knew she was right. "Don't you ever do anything that foolish again," he snarled.

"Why aren't you happy for me?" Cora demanded.

Ronan huffed and paced back and forth. "I don't know. I just didn't expect you to do something this reckless." He paused, seeing her looking away, trying to fight back the tears. Ronan let out a long sigh. "I'm glad you're okay," he said, pulling her in for a hug.

She smiled and leaned into him, letting her thoughts settle. "Warren left," she stated.

"What?" Ronan said, pulling back.

"He went to study to be a priest," Cora replied bitterly.

"It's probably for the best," Ronan remarked.

She pursed her lips and nodded. "I know."

***

Lance sat on the floor in the main common room, carefully sawing off the arm of a dead man laid out on a metal platform with holes and a tray underneath to strain the blood.

Max lounged next to them on a velvet pillow, lazily plucking a tune on his harp.

The faint scent of wet dog wafted in the air as Cora passed. Lance and Max turned to look at Cora.

"Cora!" Lance called.

"Hey!" she said, going over to them.

Max stared at her, taking in her disheveled appearance." What happened to you?" he asked.

"I killed a werewolf," she replied.

Lance stared at Cora, amazed. "How did you kill a werewolf? Tell me!" they said eagerly.

Cora smiled, exhausted. "Why don't I tell you after I've cleaned up."

"Fine," Lance grumbled, turning their attention back to peeling the flesh off the bone.

***

Cora returned, refreshed and clean. Her hair was neatly pulled back, and she had a fresh tunic on.

She sat by the body Lance was taking apart and picked up a brush. "Can I help?" she asked.

Lance nodded, grateful. "Thank you."

She began scrubbing the last remainders of blood off the freshly defleshed bones.

"Go on then," Max said, setting the harp aside. "What happened?"

"I was going to see Warren," she began. She recounted how the wolf jumped out and that she was able to stab it with her silver dagger.

"Who's Warren?" Lance asked, putting the bones in a bucket of water.

"He used to be part of my family... but not anymore." she paused, collecting her thoughts.

"What happened?" Lance asked.

"When we left the monastery, Warren came with us. He gave up the only home he knew because he was convinced he could save our souls. He thought the Bible commanded him to love others."

Lance threw their head back, laughing. "They tell you it's all about love as they're beating you with it," they scoffed.

"You were beaten with a bible too?" Cora asked, drying the bone and placing it on a cloth with the other clean ones.

Lance swallowed a lump in their throat and nodded. "Yeah. I grew up an orphan in a convent. I was told my mother had me out of wedlock and gave me up."

"I hope I'm not being rude, but...how did you turn, Lance?" she asked, changing the topic.

Lance laughed and tucked a strand of hair behind their ear. "After I left the convent, I went on to become a thief. I got very good at it. I had never once been caught until Max...."

Lance hid in the shadows of an empty ally near a tavern wearing a short black tunic and pants. The sun had just set, and there were sure to be a few wealthy merchants arriving for their evening meal.

Lance saw a person with a bulging coin purse tied to his hip approaching the tavern. The man was massive, not someone Lance wanted to get into a fight with. But hunger gnawed at their stomach.

The coin purse was hanging loosely at his side, making Lance's job easier. As the man passed, Lance silently slipped out of the shadows and quickly swiped his coin purse.

Down the alley, around the corner, and slip under the baker's fence, and they would be safe like always.

But the man began following them. Lance bristled. Stay calm, *Lance told themself.*

They managed to lose the man and made it to the fence. They quickly wriggled under the fence.

Before they could get to their feet, a large hand wrapped around their neck. Lance's gaze followed the arm up into the face of the man they had just robbed.

"Shit," Lance gasped as they were lifted off their feet. They kicked hard, then dug their nails into their captor's wrist while trying to pry his fingers off of their neck. The man was unphased. He seemed amused at Lance struggling.

Lance defiantly met the man's gaze and let out a small wheeze, surprised to see a pair of unnatural red eyes.

Their pulse quickened as panic set in. They tried to pry his hands off again, straining every muscle, but it didn't do any good.

"You shouldn't be out like this alone," the man said with a sick grin.

"No!" Lance gasped as they desperately thrashed, trying to free themselves. It was pointless. They grabbed the coin purse and held it up.

The man blinked and slightly loosened his grip, allowing Lance to speak. "You can have it back!" They said, throwing it to the side. "Please just let me go! It won't happen again. I'm sorry!"

The man blinked as he watched his coin purse drop to the ground. He set Lance on their feet but kept a firm hold on them and bent down to pick up the coin purse. "I-I didn't know it was missing. You stole this?" he asked, bewildered.

"I...uh..." Lance stammered, still struggling.

"Relax. It's all going to be okay. Just answer the question," he said gently.

Lance stopped fighting as a wave of calm swept over them. "Y-yeah. I-I s-stole it," they stammered.

"A little thing like you had quite the nerve to try to steal from someone like me," the man said sternly.

"I've never been caught before!" Lance snapped angrily.

The man raised his brows. "Never?"

"Never. And that's not going to change today," they said, drawing a knife and driving it into the man's hand.

They tried to pull away but couldn't. The man wasn't letting go. He was staring in shock at the knife sticking out of his hand.

"Well, you should be glad I'm the one who caught you," he said, dislodging the knife and throwing it to the side. "I have use for you."

He gave Lance a fanged smile.

Lance went still as their eyes flicked from the knife on the ground, to the hole in the man's hand, and to his razor-sharp teeth. There was nothing more they could think to do.

Lance's lower lip began to quiver. They looked away, mentally preparing themselves for whatever was to come next.

"What's your name?" the man said, brushing some hair out of Lance's face.

"Lance," they uttered, avoiding eye contact.

"My name's Max. I'm not going to hurt you...much." he paused. "You're of more use to me alive."

"He turned me in the alley. When I woke up, I was here. I've been here ever since," Lance finished.

"Wow…" Cora exhaled.

"That was a good night," Max said wistfully.

"For *you*," Lance quipped.

"How did you turn, Max?" Cora asked, changing the topic.

Max wilted. "Oh...where to start," he said slowly.

"You don't have to tell me. I'm sorry I asked," Cora said quickly.

"No, I want to tell you. It's been so long," he said, blinking away tears as he fidgeted with the flute he kept in his pocket. "I was married to a stunningly gorgeous woman named Hattie. Her family was wealthy. She was low ranking nobility, and I was a farmer," he chuckled, shaking his head.

"How did you marry a noble?" Cora asked.

"She loved me. I don't know how or why, but we were meant to be," he paused, smiling. "I remember the first time I saw her. She took my breath away. She was slender and had the most beautiful raven black hair. She used to sneak out of her family's estate and ride up the hills to a hidden creek. Wild berries grew there in abundance. I would go to gather them sometimes for a treat. We both ended up there at the same time, and it was love at first sight. I later learned about her rich family. We had no choice but to elope. She knew I could never give her a life of luxury, but she didn't seem to mind. We had a small vegetable farm that allowed for a comfortable living." He paused, expression darkening. "But then Lord Holward took her from me."

"William Holward?" Cora enunciated.

"No, his father, Alexander. Her parents didn't like that she ran off with me, so they made an agreement with Alexander. He would take her, make her a respectable lady, and they would double her dowry. One day he rode up and said he was taking her. I was furious and challenged him to a duel for Hattie. He was amused and agreed. That night, I lost. He left me in the field, bleeding out. When I woke up, I was here. I don't remember who turned me. I didn't really get to know them. They said that I fought well for a farmer and showed incredible bravery. Most of the vampires I knew are gone now, moved on or dead."

"I'm so sorry, Max. That must have been awful," Cora said sympathetically.

Max swallowed a lump in his throat and nodded. "Thank you." He paused. "I envy you, Cora."

She furrowed her brow and laughed nervously. "Why?"

" You've got a chance to save your brother. Very few here have had the opportunity or the ability to save their loved ones," he replied.

"I guess," Cora said slowly. "I'm not sure how he's going to feel about all this."

"I'm sure it will be fine," Max tried to reassure her.

***

Later that night, Cora sat next to her bed, watching Sam's chest rise and fall. *Everything's going to be fine,* she told herself.

Someone gently knocked on the door.

"Come in!" she called.

Ronan quietly stepped in. "There's still an hour of darkness yet. Want to go out to the stables and feed the animals?" he asked.

"Sure," she replied.

***

They sat in the barn watching the animals play with each other.

"Cora... what you did was incredible, and it worked out very well, but don't ever do anything so reckless again."

She rolled her eyes. "Fine."

"So, what's on your mind?" Ronan asked, changing the topic.

"How do I tell Sam what happened, that I'm a murderer?"

"We keep him on a need-to-know basis."

Cora looked away and nodded quietly.

"What is it?" Ronan asked, gently placing his hand on hers.

She smiled. His touch was nice. She twisted her hand to hold his. A wide smile broke across his face.

"I'm afraid he won't understand. What if he leaves like Warren did?" she asked, holding his hand tighter.

"We will work all that out when it happens," he said, giving her a tight smile.

She took a deep breath. "You're right. I shouldn't be worried yet."

"And when he does come to, we can keep him upstairs until he feels ready to go home if he chooses."

She rested her head on his shoulder, and he carefully put his arm around her.

"Thank you," she said quietly.

A cat with a blue collar that said "Isabel" pawed at Ronan's pant leg, mewling. He happily turned his attention to her.

"I know what you want," Ronan said, getting a drinking glass. He filled it with water and set it down by her. She immediately began lapping it up.

Cora looked at Ronan, confused. "She will only drink water if it's in a drinkin' glass. Don't ask me why. I don't understand her," he explained.

Cora chuckled. "Did you make those collars for them?"

"Yeah," he admitted sheepishly.

"So they're your pets?" she asked.

Ronan shrugged. "I like to think of em' that way."

A cat with a grey collar trotted up to Isabel. "Sterling, don't," Ronan said sternly.

Sterling cocked his head to the side and knocked over Isabel's drinking glass. Isabel hissed. Sterling ran off, Isabel chasing after him.

Ronan sighed and shook his head. Cora laughed, some of her worries finally melting away.

Chapter Eleven
The day before the full moon

Cora spent the next day getting things ready for Sam. After sunrise, she ventured out, making sure to keep her covered in her red cloak. She had a spring in her step that wasn't there before as she thought about how she would get to see Sam awake later. It wasn't long before she arrived at her old house. She paused outside, hand hovering over the knob.

She sniffled and pushed the door open, stepping inside. For a moment, a sense of comforting familiarity rushed through her. Cora wanted to hang onto the feeling, but it was quickly washed away by reality. Everything was still and quiet.

Normally at this time, Warren would be awake and on his way to the farm, he worked at.

Her heart ached as the memories flashed through her mind. It was all gone. She forced each step as she went into the bedroom.

She leaned against the wall and sank to the floor, sobbing. She missed Warren. She wanted the comforting routine back. But that was all lost.

There was still so much to do, and the full moon was tomorrow. She forced herself to her feet and collected Sam's clothes from the trunk by the foot of the bed. She grabbed his hunting knife and the brass candle holder that belonged to their mothers.

There was nothing left for her here. Slowly she trudged out the door into the morning sun. The warmth seeped through her cloak. She sighed and wiped the last tears away.

She had a new family, and Sam was waiting back at Nightwoods castle. A sad smile formed on her lips, and she broke into a sprint. The cool breeze felt nice against her face as she raced through the woods.

Shortly after, she arrived at the castle, then headed immediately to her room downstairs. Sam was lying in bed, sleeping peacefully. She began putting his books on the bookshelf and put his clothes in the trunk. When she stepped back and admired the room, it felt a little like home.

Cora gently kissed Sam's forehead and went back out onto the common area.

The night of the full moon

Cora ran up to Ronan excitedly, nearly tripping over herself. "It's the full moon!"

Ronan put the book down and slowly nodded. "It is."

"How do I do this?" she asked, bouncing slightly.

Ronan chuckled. He had never seen her this excited. The way her smile lit up her face warmed the pit of his stomach. "First thing's first, we've got to get him outside," Ronan said, standing.

He scooped Sam in his arms and carried him out into the moonlight. They leaned him against the stone wall of the castle. Ronan took out a small book from his cloak and flipped to a page in the middle. "Say these words while you drink. The rest should come naturally.," he said, pointing to the text and handing it to her.

"That's it?" she asked, scanning the page. "There's nothing more?"

"Nothing more. You have to mean it, though," he explained.

She paused as a pang of anxiety hit her. "What if it doesn't work?" she asked.

"Then we will keep tryin' until something does work," Ronan replied.

She let out a nervous breath. "With the moon as my witness, I make this promise: as long as you are mine, I will bleed for thee, Sam Mason," she recited, sinking her teeth into his neck. She carefully drank, feeling a part of his flow into her.

Her mind quieted as an image formed in her mind. Sam was lying in bed while Warren spoon-fed him. "I'm so sick of this!" Warren complained. "I can't keep doing it."

He went on and on lamenting how hard he had it while Sam was helpless in bed, embarrassed, furious, and ashamed.

The image faded, and a new one came into view. She saw an old man standing over Sam with a bottle of holy water sprinkling on his head. "I baptize you in the name of the father and the son and the holy spirit," the man said.

She could feel the pain in Sam's chest as his heart shattered and his anger at being so helpless.

A jolt of hope surged through Cora as she felt his pulse get stronger.

Sam's eyes flew open, and he gasped. A pinching in his neck brought him to the present. Someone was biting him. He burst into tears as he struggled to breathe. *Please let this be the end!*

The person released his neck and looked at him.

"Sam,. It's okay," a familiar voice said.

Sam didn't register what was happening. He slumped over and cried onto the person's shoulder. Frustration coursed through his body as he wept.

"Sam," the person pulled back and held him in place.

Sam saw a pair of red eyes looking back at him. He let out a small nervous breath.

"Sam," a familiar voice said. "It's me."

Sam squinted and recognized who had bitten him. "Cora," he wheezed. "Cora!" He said again. He threw his arms around her pulling her in for a tight hug. He froze with his arms around her. He was surprised his body had listened to him. Surprised he'd heard his own voice after so long.

Cora hugged him back. "Hey," she choked as happy tears spilled over.

"Cora," he repeated. His heart clenched hearing his own voice again. It was starting to sound familiar.

Sam broke down in gut-wrenching sobs. It felt good to feel again. Even the pain of coming alive. He laughed as he struggled to breathe. Despite his scattered thoughts, he was sharper than ever. He was there. He was present.

Sam pulled back and studied her. She was still Cora, but her eyes were bright red, and her skin an ashen grey color.

He noticed the two blood-stained fangs in her toothy grin.

"What happened?" he sputtered, stumbling to his feet. Cora grabbed his arm to keep him from falling over.

"Your teeth! Your eyes! What's happening?" he stammered, terrified.

"It's okay, Sam," Cora said gently. "I'm going to explain everything."

He reached up to feel the puncture wounds in his neck. "W-what did you do to me?" he asked, stepping back.

She quickly retracted her fangs and took a step towards him. "You don't have to be afraid, Sam. I'm still me."

"What's happening?" he asked, taking another step back, bumping into someone. He looked up to see another pair of red eyes. This person had red hair, and their skin was as pale as Cora's.

"I suppose I should introduce myself," Ronan said, giving Sam some room.

"W-who are you?" Sam uttered.

Ronan slowly stepped around Sam, so he was facing him, and extended his hand. "My name's Ronan."

"S-sam," he stuttered, not moving to take it.

Ronan withdrew his hand.

"What happened?" Sam asked desperately.

"Cora made a deal with me. She had angered Lord Holward, and he was goin' to kill her in the morning," Ronan began.

Sam blinked away tears. "I remember that...."

"I told her that if she allowed me to turn her, we would help you," Ronan explained.

"Turned into what?"

"A vampire," Ronan laughed. "But then she got herself bitten by a werewolf and turned into a vayer so she could take your soul and give you immortality."

"A werewolf! Immortality! What?"

"I know this is a lot," Cora said, putting a gentle hand on his shoulder.

Sam shrank back as his heart slammed in his chest.

"We should probably get you into some clean clothes," Cora said.

"Where's Warren?" Sam asked, looking down.

"Oh," Cora said, deflating. "He left. He was convinced I was possessed, and he went to seminary."

Sam laughed and shook his head. "No, he didn't. He left because of me."

"What?" Cora uttered.

"Every damn day, I heard him go on and on about how much he hated me. He was angry because I wasn't getting better, and he was the one who had to deal with me. He said he shouldn't have to deal with the consequences of my sin," he said, voice shaking. "I know he didn't think I could understand. But I heard and understood every word!" he paused. "I was still there."

Cora looked down as she processed what was said.

"I'm glad he's gone! Good riddance!" Sam spat.

Cora clenched her hands into fists as she gritted her teeth.

Sam went quiet and wilted as more memories came back.

"Sam?" Cora said hesitantly.

"He had me baptized," Sam uttered.

"He what?" Cora exploded.

"He had me baptized," Sam repeated quietly. "He had a priest come by, and they prayed for me and baptized me."

A tear rolled down his cheek. "And I couldn't do anything. He knew I didn't want that! And yet he did it anyway!" Sam continued.

Cora was visibly shaking with fury. Ronan put a hand on her shoulder. "We can kill Warren later if you like," he whispered, quiet enough so that Sam couldn't hear.

"I'll consider it," she said, shaking him off. "We need to focus on Sam now."

"What's going on?" Sam asked.

"We're going to get you something to eat and clean clothes. And then we'll go from there," she said with a warm smile.

"Hello!" Lance said, appearing next to Sam.

"What the hell?" Sam yelped, stumbling back. Cora caught his arm to steady him. "Where did you come from? Who *are* you?"

"My name's Lance, and you're Sam," they said, holding out a basket of pastries. "This is for you. I stole it."

"From where?" Sam asked slowly.

"The baker in town," Lance said with a sly smile.

Cora groaned and shook her head.

Sam hesitantly took the basket. "Uh...t-thank you," he stammered.

"We have a room ready for you," Lance said excitedly.

"Upstairs, right?" Cora said firmly.

Lance nodded. "Come in when you're ready!" they said, running off.

Ronan shook his head. "I am so sorry about Lance; they can be a bit…."

"Adorable!" Sam finished, taking a bite of a pastry.

Cora laughed. "Let's go inside."

Sam exhaled as a wave of exhaustion swept through him. He threw his arm around her shoulders to keep from falling.

"Are you okay?" she asked.

"Ugh. I'm still tired," Sam seethed, angry at his weakness.

"Let's get you inside," she said, letting him lean on her for support as they went in.

He sat on the bench by the long wooden table and picked a pastry from the basket Lance had given him.

They sat in silence while he ate. Sam relished every bite. He flexed his fingers and smiled.

"There's something else you need to know," she said hesitantly.

"And what's that?" Sam asked.

Cora took a deep breath. "I need to drink blood to survive. Human blood."

Sam's head snapped up, and he stared at her wide-eyed. "W-what?" he stammered.

"I've done a lot of bad things since coming here," she continued.

"Like what?" Sam asked.

"I've killed people," she said slowly.

"You've killed people?" Sam repeated.

Cora looked away, ashamed, and nodded. "I need their blood to survive," she stated.

Sam took a shaky breath and rested his head on the table, trying to sort out his tangled thoughts.

Cora nervously fidgeted with a strand of hair.

"What about Lance and Ronan? Are they...killers too?" Sam asked, not looking at her.

Cora nodded again and pursed her lips. "We all are," she choked.

Sam put his head in his hands and tried to slow down his thoughts.

A few tears rolled down Cora's face. "Sam, I am so sorry. I know this is a lot," she said, voice rough from holding back her emotions.

"How many?" Sam asked coldly.

"How many what?" she asked.

"How many have you murdered?" he questioned sharply.

"I-I don't know, Sam. I don't keep count," she stammered.

Sam clenched his jaw until his teeth hurt. This was all too much. He forced back the bile that had risen in his throat at the thought of his sister killing people. He couldn't picture it. She's still Cora, he reminded himself, pushing away the knowledge that the old Cora was gone.

"Sam, this was the only way to get you back," she said desperately.

"I never left!" he snapped.

Cora wiped her eyes. "I'm sorry," she whimpered, looking away. "You don't have to stay if you don't want to."

"I'm not leaving you," Sam sighed.

"Promise?"

"Yes," he said firmly.

She smiled sadly. "Thank you."

"How do you do it? Is it quick and painless?" Sam asked, changing the topic.

"Of course!" she lied.

Sam looked away and pursed his lips. He leaned over and put his head in his hands as he thought out how to go forward.

She's a killer...but still my sister. I'm going to stay for her. I have to.

"Cora, I'm so grateful for what you've done. And I'm not leaving you. You're my sister," he stated flatly.

She smiled sadly. "Thank you, Sam."

"So, where are you staying?" Sam inquired.

"Just downstairs," she said quickly.

"Can I see?" he asked. "I want to make sure they're treating my sister right."

"I'm not sure that's such a good idea," she said slowly.

"Please," he begged. "If I'm going to be staying here, I want to know my way around."

Cora took a deep breath. "Alright, but it may be a bit much."

"I understand," Sam replied.

She gently took him by the hand and led him to the bedroom with the hidden stairs. "Are you sure about this?" she asked, glancing nervously at him.

"Yes. I need to know. I'm done being kept on the outside of things. I'm not a child. I can handle this!" he said, voice rising.

"Alright," Cora said, putting her hand on his shoulder.

He let out a calming breath. "Thank you."

She slowly opened the door. Lance was sitting cross-legged on the bed, carving something from a bone.

Their eyes lit up when they saw Sam, and they jumped off the bed. "Hi!" they said, landing lightly in front of Sam. "Here." They held out a small circular bone with an intricate swirl design etched in around a ruby.

Cora held her breath as Sam took it. "W-what is this?" he stammered.

"It's a worry bone," Lance stated proudly. "I have one too!" They said, holding up one similar. "It helps me focus."

Sam stared at it blankly. He ran his thumb over the gem and swirls. "Is this made from a human bone?" He asked slowly.

"Yeah," Lance said, their smile fading.

Sam took a deep breath as he absentmindedly fiddled with it. "Thank you," he uttered.

Lance's smile returned, and Sam couldn't help but smile back. "Uh..what should I expect?" he asked.

Cora opened her mouth to speak, but Lance cut her off. "It's beautiful! I've always been pretty good at carving. I made a few good weapons in my human years. They let me decorate with bones I carved," Lance said, beaming proudly.

Sam went quiet, looking at the small trinket in his hand. It belonged to someone. A human like him. This was the price he had to pay to be with his sister, who gave up nearly everything for him.

He forced a tight smile. "I can't wait to see it."

Lance grinned and lifted the bed revealing the staircase. They gracefully bowed, signaling for Sam and Cora to go ahead.

Sam gripped the small gift as he followed his sister down the stairs. Lance hopped down the stairs behind them.

"I made those!" Lance said, proudly pointing to a set of chairs. "Lemme show you!" Lance took Sam's hand and led him to the chairs.

Cora followed closely.

Lance excitedly talked about all the little details they added to the chair they were proud of.

"I also made that!" Lance said, pointing to a large chandelier.

"You made that?" Sam sputtered.

"Yep," Lance said.

"It's beautiful," Sam uttered.

"I want to show you more!" Lance said. They had Sam sit at one of the tables as they skipped off.

Sam chuckled.

Cora sighed and shook her head. "I'm sorry about Lance."

"Why?" Sam asked. "I like him."

"Them," Lance corrected, returning and laying small trinkets on the table.

"Them?" Sam clarified.

"Yep," Lance replied.

They excitedly talked about each trinket and how they made them. Sam struggled to pay attention and rested his head on his hand, fighting to stay awake.

"Sam, are you okay?" Cora asked.

"Peachy," Sam said coldly.

"You're still human. You need to sleep," she said, putting a gentle hand on his shoulder.

"No!" Sam snapped, pulling away. "I don't want to go back! I don't want to be sick again!"

Cora tilted her head to the side, confused. "You won't...."

"I've done nothing but lay in bed for a year!" He sputtered. " I can't...I can't..." Sam struggled for air as his head spun. He reached for the worry bone and ran his thumb over it, focusing on how it felt. "I'm still broken!" he said angrily.

Cora tried to think of something to say but came up empty. She buried her face in her hands and sighed.

Lance saw what happened and walked over to them. "I will wake you! How long?" they said.

Sam looked at them, confused.

"Six hours? Four Hours?" Lance smiled expectantly, eager for Sam's answer.

Sam felt a little better at the thought of being able to have a say in how long he sleeps. "4."

"Okay," Lance said, gently guiding him to his feet.

Sam leaned on them as they helped him to bed.

***

Cora went out to the barn as the sun began to set. She snuggled Bruce and watched the animals play.

Ronan appeared next to her and sat. "Are you alright?" he asked.

"Did I do the right thing?" she asked, burying her face in Bruce's fur.

"Of course you did," Ronan said, putting a comforting hand on her shoulder.

She leaned into him, and he closed his arms around her, holding her close. "I have never seen such bravery and selflessness from anyone," he said, gently brushing a tear from her cheek.

"What if he can't be happy here? What if I've ruined everything for him?" she stammered.

"Cora, you just took his soulless than a day ago. Give it time," he said.

She laughed bitterly. "I suppose you're right," she said. But she couldn't push away a small twinge of guilt that gnawed at her insides.

***

4 hours passed, and Lance quietly slipped into Sam's room. He laid in the bed, sleeping peacefully. Lance had to stifle a small squeak seeing how perfect Sam was. They smiled, seeing how different he looked sleeping this time. He looked younger and more relaxed. They brushed a strand of hair out of his eyes.

They hovered over Sam and gently poked his shoulder. "Sam, wake up," Lance said.

Sam opened his eyes slowly to see Lance's face inches from his. His heart slammed in his chest, and he blushed fiercely.

Lance grinned. "Good morning!" they chirped.

"Yep," Sam replied stiffly.

Lance helped him sit up. "How do you feel?" They asked.

"Tired but good," Sam said, reaching to throw the cover off, but their hand brushed across Lance's hand.

Heat rose to Lance's face as they smiled, feeling Sam's hand on theirs. A wave of chills swept through them, washing away any warmth. They didn't care. They wanted to stay like this with Sam.

"Are you okay?" Sam asked, feeling the drop in temperature of Lance's skin.

They sighed and nodded. "I need blood."

"You should get some," Sam said slowly.

"Will you be okay?" Lance asked. "I don't want to leave you."

"I'll be okay," Sam replied gratefully.

"Why don't I show you where to get food," Cora suggested.

Lance gave Sam a quick hug before leaving.

Cora led him upstairs to the kitchen. There was a large pantry filled with cheese, salted meats, and jams.

"Are you sure I can just...take food like this?" Sam asked.

"As long as you don't take too much," Cora said.

Sam took some cheese and salted meat off the shelf, and they sat in the servant's dining hall. Sam ate quietly, glaring at a stain on the table as if it were the devil.

"So...uh...did you sleep well?" Cora asked, trying to make casual conversation.

"Nope," Sam said, bluntly not taking his eyes off the stain.

"Are you mad at me?" Cora asked, shrinking back.

Sam shook his head and swallowed the bite of cheese. "No. I'm mad at everyone else. For almost two years, I was an object. I couldn't do anything." He said, voice rising. He paused and took a calming breath. "But you saw me as a person. You didn't give up on me. Of course, I'm not mad at you."

Cora smiled sadly.

"Do you still have that top Warren and I gave you?"

Cora looked away as her heart broke. "No...I'm so sorry. I lost it. Why do you ask?"

Sam shrugged and took another bite. "I just want something to do," he said, taking out the worry bone.

"I'm sorry," she said. "I really tried to find it. I looked everywhere."

"It's okay, Cora," he said, looking at her with tired eyes. "I'm sure we can have another one made."

Lance re-joined them after they finished eating. They slid on the bench next to Sam. "Hi," they said excitedly.

Sam groaned, frustrated as the room spun. He didn't want to sleep again.

"Are you tired again?" Lance asked, furrowing their brow concerned.

Sam nodded angrily.

"I'll wake you up like last time," Lance said. "How long do you want to sleep?"

Sam went quiet, thinking. "5 hours," he said.

Epilogue
One Year Later

Lance paced nervously outside Sam's room, holding a small gift for Sam.

His door had a sign with a red x painted on one side to show he was sleeping and didn't want to be disturbed. The other side had a white circle to show that he was awake, and they could knock if they needed him.

"Come on," Lance said, impatiently tapping their foot.

"What are you doing?" Cora asked from behind them.

Lance spun on their heels to face her. "It's his first anniversary of coming to live with us, and I made him this!" They held out a small decorative apple carved from bone and encrusted in rubies. "And I want him to wake up so I can give it to him." Lance paused and looked at the apple. "Do you think he'll like it?"

Cora smiled and nodded. "He will like it a lot more if he gets a full night's rest."

Lance sighed.

The door slowly opened, and Sam stepped out, messy hair and bleary-eyed. Lance smiled and threw their arms around his middle.

Sam tried to blink the sleep out of his eyes, smiling at Lance. He brought his arms around them and hugged them tightly.

Lance pulled back and gave Sam the decorative apple. "You have been here a whole year. This is for you," they said, handing it to Sam.

"Lance, this is beautiful! You made this?" Sam asked.

Lance smiled proudly and nodded.

Sam swept them up in a hug.

Cora snorted. Lance looked so tiny in Sam's arms despite being a thousand times stronger. "My turn," she said, holding up a large brown bag.

Sam allowed himself a moment more to enjoy Lance in his arms before letting go.

Cora handed him the bag. "It's from me and Ronan," she said.

Sam opened it, and inside was a bow and a set of silver-tipped arrows. Sam's face lit up as he struggled to find words. "Thank you!" he said, setting it aside and hugging her.

"Thank you for staying," she whispered.

"Thank you for making me better," Sam responded.

"Come on, Sam," Lance said, bouncing slightly. "I wanna see you shoot!"

They took Sam by the hand and led him away. "I haven't done this before!" Sam protested.

"Then I can watch you learn!" Lance chirped excitedly.

As they ran off, Cora grinned. Seeing Sam and Lance's relationship develop over the past year, watching Sam's happiness grow, made everything else worthwhile.